SCANDAL

SCANDAL

A NOVEL BY

KATE BRIAN

SIMON & SCHUSTER BFYR

New York   London   Toronto   Sydney

SIMON & SCHUSTER BFYR

An imprint of Simon & Schuster Children's Publishing Division
1230 Avenue of the Americas, New York, NY 10020

SIMON & SCHUSTER BFYR

is a trademark of Simon & Schuster, Inc.

For information about special discounts for bulk purchases, please contact
Simon & Schuster Special Sales at 1-866-506-1949 or
business@simonandschuster.com.
The Simon & Schuster Speakers Bureau can bring authors to your live
event. For more information or to book an event, contact the Simon &
Schuster Speakers Bureau at 1-866-248-3049 or visit our website
at www.simonspeakers.com.

alloyentertainment
Produced by Alloy Entertainment
151 West 26th Street, New York, NY 10001

Typography by Andrea C. Uva
The text of this book was set in Filosofia.
Manufactured in the United States of America
2 4 6 8 10 9 7 5 3
Library of Congress Control Number 2009941645
ISBN 978-1-4169-8470-2
ISBN 978-1-4169-9905-8 (eBook)

For my little sister, because I hope she'll find this in a faraway bookstore and know I was thinking of her

SCANDAL

COME TOGETHER

We came from all corners of campus. From Pemberly, from Bradwell, from Parker. Some came in pairs. Others alone. Some defiant, with heads held high. Others meek, with curled shoulders, books clutched to their chests. Salt crunched beneath our feet. The frigid New England wind bit at our noses. Our fingers stung inside fur-lined gloves. In the silence, we came together, ignoring the curious stares of students who hustled by. Ignoring the whispers, the snickers, the scoffs. We waited for the last of us to arrive, each searching the other faces. Each unsure of what to do next. Of where we belonged. Of who we were.

For the Billings Girls, this was not a familiar sensation.

But it was familiar to me. Because not that long ago I'd been Reed Brennan, Glass-Licker, the New Girl. The awkward scholarship student from a no-name town in Pennsylvania. Not that long ago I'd been no one, and I'd handled it. Which might have been why, after a few moments of tense silence, everyone looked at me, as if searching for guidance.

"Well," I said. "This sucks."

Constance Talbot and Lorna Gross laughed. Kiki Rosen smirked. Missy Thurber and Shelby Wordsworth rolled their eyes. Tiffany Goulbourne lifted her ever-present camera and snapped some rapid-fire photos of our strained faces. Everyone else seemed to relax, shoulders lowering, postures unclenching. Maybe it was my joke, or maybe they just didn't want to look pinched and tense in the pictures.

"Tiffany, is that really necessary?" Shelby asked, lifting a hand to the camera as if Tiff were a stalkerazzi.

"Just making memories," Tiff said.

"Why would you want to remember this?" Portia Ahronian tilted her head ever so slightly toward the north side of campus, where the tall tower of Billing House once loomed. All that was left was a huge dirt patch, currently being flattened by a yellow bulldozer. The machinery groaned and creaked, and just as the huge shovel-thing at the front lowered to the ground with a bang, Gage Coolidge and a few of his more obnoxious friends let out a whoop and a cheer.

"Dude! Nothing like a little destruction to start the new year!" Gage cackled as he walked by us from the direction of the boys' dorms. He had a skullcap pulled low over his brow and his irritatingly handsome face was covered in stubble. As animated as he was, his eyes were rimmed in red, like he'd just gotten home from partying. Which he probably had. Wherever Gage went, he took the party with him. At least, so he liked to think.

"You're such an ass," Astrid Chou snapped at him.

"Ooh. Frisky," Gage replied, looking her up and down. He licked his lips in a way that made me want to lop his tongue off. "Wanna stay in my room tonight? I mean, since you no longer have one."

Astrid rolled her eyes and Gage's friends slapped him on the back, laughing as they shoved their way into the cafeteria.

"That boy needs a lobotomy," Tiffany said.

"Doesn't a lobotomy require a brain to remove?" I joked.

At that moment, Noelle Lange finally graced us with her presence. She walked up, her dark hair billowing in the breeze, her black coat buttoned all the way up to her chin.

"In case you people haven't noticed, it's freezing out here," she said with a sniff. I tried to meet her eyes to see what she was thinking, but her Gucci sunglasses were so dark all I could see was my own reflection and the gray clouds gathering over our heads. "Let's go."

She opened the double doors to the dining hall and in we walked, turning our backs on the empty space that was Billings. We moved in a pack, like a class of suburban kindergartners shuffling through a museum in the big city, sticking close for safety. As we entered the cavernous room, the walls of gray brick matching the sky outside, the place fell eerily silent. And just like that, our brief moment of levity was over.

Everyone was watching us—students, teachers, food service workers. It was the first Monday morning of the new semester and all anyone could think about, talk about, care about was the fact that Billings was no more. Once the most popular and powerful girls on campus, we were now the train wreck from which no one could look away.

We passed my friend Marc Alberro's table, and he shot me a sympathetic look, but I had to wonder if he was also taking mental notes for some human-interest piece for the student paper. Diana Waters and Sonal Shah whispered behind their hands and I felt a niggling sense of paranoia. I lifted my hand in a wave, trying to show them I was okay—that there was nothing worth whispering about—but I couldn't even muster a smile to go with it. I wasn't okay. I felt like my stomach had turned to Jell-O inside me, all quivery and unfirm. Then Constance linked her arm with mine and I took a breath. I still had my friends. And our usual tables in the center of the room were still waiting for us. That was something, at least.

When we sat, chatter started up again. Plates clinked, knives scraped. I felt like collapsing forward on the table and taking a nap. Or crying. Or both. Which was, perhaps, what the general population of Easton Academy was expecting us all to do. Break down. Show a crack in our perfect exteriors.

Not this Billings Girl, though. Jell-O might have been taking over my insides, but my outsides were going to stay intact.

"I can't believe Billings is gone," London Simmons said.

Right. Putting it out of my mind wasn't going to be an option.

"I mean, it's just . . . *gone*," she repeated. Her highlighted brown hair was down around her face and her lashes were so long and thick they made her eyes look huge. Her purple turtleneck grazed her chin but was tight enough to show off all her curvaceous assets.

"We went over there this morning to see if we could grab a brick or something. You know, as a memento?" Vienna Clarke added, leaning forward on the table. She could have passed for London's double, but with slightly less makeup. "There was *nothing* there."

"It's like it never existed at all," Amberly Carmichael confirmed, bringing both hands under her chin. The belled sleeves of her pink angora sweater were pulled down to her fingertips, and her long blond hair was slicked back under a matching pink headband.

"Don't say that," Missy snapped, her wide nostrils flaring. "Billings has been part of this community for over a hundred years. We have to keep its memory alive, at least."

My heart squeezed. I'd never heard Missy sound so impassioned about anything—even Billings. Even if it was bitchily impassioned.

"What're we going to do?" Rose Sakowitz asked. She looked tiny and meek at the far end of the second table, cuddled into a huge white sweater, her red hair drawn into a low ponytail. "I mean, we can't live like this, all split up."

"They put me back in Bradwell," Amberly muttered. "My old roommate, Cassie, has had a single since I moved to Billings. She was *not* happy to see me."

Everyone had received their new room assignments in their mailboxes the day before. The administration had not only scattered the Billings Girls over three dorms, but they'd separated roommates, just for kicks. Portia and Tiffany were now living together in Parker, along with the random pairings of Rose and Astrid, London and Shelby, and Kiki and Vienna. In Pemberly, Lorna and Constance were living together, while Noelle and Missy each had singles there, like me. I'd been placed there last semester when the Billings Girls had thrown me out of the house for betraying Noelle—a crime of which I'd since been absolved—so I was the only one of us who didn't have to move.

"Our room doesn't even have a view," Portia said, glancing at Tiffany.

"We're looking out at the Dumpsters behind the gym," Tiff confirmed, sticking her tongue out slightly.

"And the closets? They don't even hold my coats," Portia, added, flicking her long dark hair over one shoulder. "I mean, WTF? What did we do to deserve this?"

"Nothing," Astrid put in. She'd dyed the tips of her black hair white and had on more green eyeliner than strictly necessary. But as always, it worked for her. "It's bollocks. This is the school's fault, not ours. They're the ones who let loony Ariana Osgood and her half-baked sister Sabine in here in the first place. Why should we be punished because their admissions process is total shite?"

Everyone muttered their agreement, shifting in their seats, getting riled up.

"We have to do something, right?" Shelby said. Her dark blond hair was pinned back in a prim bun and she wore a houndstooth jacket over a white T-shirt and pearls. As always, her iPhone was out and vibrating on the table in front of her. "I mean, this is my senior year. I can't spend the rest of it living in that . . . *hovel*." She gave a shudder. "It's completely ridiculous."

"It's like we're not even us anymore," Constance said.

"Noelle, you have a plan, right?" London asked, biting her bottom lip.

Thirteen pairs of desperate eyes turned to Noelle. She removed her sunglasses slowly, folded them, and placed them on the table in front of her. She laid both hands flat over the frames for a moment as she took a breath. When she lifted her eyes, she looked around the two tables. A tingle of excitement raced down my spine. Whatever Noelle had in mind, it was going to be good. I could feel it.

"Ladies," she said. "It's time to move on."

"What?" I blurted, voicing the sentiments of every shocked person in earshot.

Noelle looked me dead in the eye, her brown bangs swept sideways like a curtain drawn over her face. "This is it. Billings, as we know it, is gone. We're going to have to accept it."

I felt as if my chair was shaking beneath me. Then I realized it was me. I was trembling in my seat.

"Don't say that," I replied. "It can't be over. There has to be something we can do."

"Like what?" Noelle said, arching one perfect eyebrow. "What're you going to do, little piggy? Build a new house out of straw?"

I clutched the edge of the table. What was wrong with her? London was right. Noelle was always in charge. She always, *always* had a plan. And Billings House meant more to her than anyone else at these two tables. Of that I was certain. How could she possibly be giving up so easily?

"She's right, Reed," Tiffany said, leaning back in her chair. "The house is gone. I think this is going to be a tough one to overcome, even for you."

My heart started to sink, but I yanked it up again. A tough one even for me? The girl whose boyfriend had been murdered by one of her best friends? The girl who'd almost been shot less than a month ago? The girl who'd been stranded on a deserted island for a week and left for dead?

If I could handle all that, how could I *not* handle this?

"No," I said. "This is not over."

"Reed," Noelle said in a condescending voice, "there's this little thing called knowing when to quit. A smart person can see a lost cause by daylight."

"Well then call me an idiot, because I'm not giving up," I replied, crossing my arms over my chest. "Billings is my home. Our home. I'm not letting it go that easily."

Come on, Noelle. Say you're with me on this. You have to be.

But Noelle scoffed and shoved back from the table. "I'm getting a bagel," she said as she stood. "Anyone else want to join me over here in Realityville?"

Ever so slowly, they started to follow. Portia, Shelby, Vienna, London, Amberly. They shot me sad, sorry looks as they trailed after her.

Fine. Let them follow her—for now. I was going to prove her wrong. Somehow, I was going to convince them. I looked around at the rest of my friends, most of whom were now eyeing me with nervous hope. Somehow, I was going to bring us all back together.

And for maybe the second time in her life, Noelle Lange was going to have to admit that she was wrong.

HOPE AND CHANGE

I tried not to look at the Billings destruction site as I crossed the snow-covered campus with Constance, Kiki, and Astrid, all of us huddled together against the cold, rushing for the stone chapel on the east side of the quad. Once inside, I was hit with a surprisingly warm wall of air. I tugged off my wool hat and looked at my friends in confusion.

"It's like the Caribbean in here," Constance said, removing her red wool gloves.

The Caribbean. Sigh. Even though I'd sworn I'd never go back there, the word instantly conjured up thoughts of Upton Giles, my winter break boyfriend, and my heart pinged and panged like mad. I could practically feel his solid arms around me, smell the clean island scent of him in the air. I wondered what he was doing right then. Oxford was five hours ahead, so he might very well have been heading off to class at the university, lunching with friends, or catching up on his reading for school. I imagined what he might say to me if he knew about Billings.

"It's your future, Reed. Your choice. Who are you going to be?"

I felt a shiver as his sexy English accent echoed in my mind. Later I'd give him a call and a chance to pep-talk me himself.

"Reed? People are starting to queue up," Astrid said, nudging me from behind. Her English accent wasn't quite as hot as Upton's, but it got me moving.

I shed my coat and let the other girls slide into one of the pews ahead of me so I could sit on the end. The source of all the unexpected warmth appeared to be a series of long white space heaters, which had been placed along the outer walls of the chapel. Their insides glowed red and filled the air with the nose-prickling scent of warm iron. Why no one had ever thought of this before was beyond me. It gave the formerly cold, dank chapel a pleasant, cozy vibe. Many of the students around me actually looked happy to be there. That was new.

The whispering and chatter suddenly intensified and I turned around to find Spencer Hathaway walking into the chapel, along with his two sons Sawyer and Graham. Graham, all preppy in a burgundy V-neck sweater and navy pea coat, took a seat at the very back of the chapel in the senior section. Sawyer and his dad paused at the end of the pew across from mine and whispered a few words to each other; then Sawyer sat as his dad made his way up the aisle to the podium. As soon as Mr. Hathaway got there, the chapel fell silent. In his seat, Sawyer flicked his blond hair away from his eyes. I waved and his entire demeanor relaxed when he saw me.

"How are you?" he mouthed.

I shrugged. "Fine, I guess."

"Good morning, Easton Academy students!" Mr. Hathaway's voice boomed across the chapel, scaring my heart into a sprint. I saw Lorna and Missy exchange an incredulous look. Who knew such a commanding voice could come out of such a slight, handsome man? The few people who hadn't been at attention before were now.

Astrid whistled quietly. "The new headmaster is *hotttt*!" she sang.

"Ew," I replied under my breath. "He's, like, over forty."

"And *hot*!"

I stifled a laugh and faced forward. I guess when it came to parental types, Mr. Hathaway was on the good-looking side. He was of medium height, no taller than I was, but slim and athletic. He wore his dark hair slicked back from his face, and his pin-striped suit was slim-cut and stylish.

"My name is Headmaster Hathaway," he said, resting his hands on either side of the podium.

"Double H. I like it. Very sexy superspy," Astrid said.

"Where do you come up with these things?" I whispered.

"I have a highly creative inner dialogue running through my head at all times," she replied matter-of-factly.

"I'm here to welcome you to a brand-new semester and a brand-new era, at Easton Academy," Headmaster Hathaway continued.

"Oh boy. Here we go," Kiki said sarcastically, slumping so low in her seat her butt hung off the pew. "Hope and change all over again. I get the appeal, but the coattails are full. Get a new point of view already."

"I'm sure you've all noticed there have been a few changes around here since you've been gone." Headmaster Hathaway smoothed his eggplant-colored tie and drew himself up straight, like he was preening over the destruction of Billings. Which kind of made me want to smack him.

Kiki rolled her eyes at me and mouthed "duh."

"In addition to the obvious, physical changes to the campus, I'd like to mention one new rule up front," he said, pacing out from behind the podium. "As of today, elitism and insularity will no longer be tolerated at Easton Academy. Any and all social groups and clubs are to be disbanded, and no new clubs will be incorporated unless they have a clear mission statement. In order to facilitate this change, any new clubs will have to fill out an application in my office, which will be reviewed by me personally."

Here he paused, to level us all with a no-nonsense stare. I didn't know of any clubs on campus that were strictly social clubs, so I wasn't sure whom he was trying to intimidate.

"I want you to know that while some of these changes may seem, at the moment, unfair, they were all made in your interest—and in the interest of the community of Easton Academy at large. I have been brought here by your board of directors to usher in a new way of thinking," he said, clasping his hands. "I value honesty, integrity, humility, and, above all else, equality."

I swallowed hard. Was Mr. Hathaway saying what I thought he was saying? Had it been his decision to tear down Billings to send a message? To put us all on the same level? I glanced over at Sawyer, but he was staring ahead, studiously avoiding my gaze.

"But I also value your opinions," the headmaster said, seeming somehow to make eye contact with each of the two hundred–plus students in the room. "This is your school. It should be a place where you feel nurtured, inspired, and safe."

I looked down the pew at my friends. Safe was one thing I hadn't felt around here in a long time. Around the room, people sat up a bit straighter, looked at one another, impressed. Hathaway already had them eating out of his hand.

"To that end, I will have an open-door policy," Mr. Hathaway continued. "If you have any questions about the changes being made on campus, please feel free to stop by my office to chat. My goal is to get to know every one of you personally. The better we know one another, the better we can work together."

A bright smile creased Headmaster Hathaway's tan face. I had definitely liked Sawyer's dad when we were all down in St. Barths together, and he still seemed like a vast improvement over Headmaster Cromwell, who was more like an automaton than a person, but there was something about his touchy-feely speech that made my skin crawl. I wanted a headmaster, not a new BFF or therapist.

"But this semester won't be *all* about work," he said, relaxing his posture and giving us a grin. "A week from Saturday I will be hosting a schoolwide party in the Great Room. A get-to-know-you dance of sorts. It's going to be a lot of fun and I expect to see all of you there."

A dubious murmur carried throughout the room. No one at Easton attended on-campus school dances. Unless they were clueless. Or freshmen. Or were, you know, dared to go, as I had been last year by Missy and Lorna for the first dance of my sophomore year.

Of course, I'd ended up sharing my first kiss with Thomas Pearson at that dance, so, as lame as it had been, it was one of my best nights at Easton. I hugged my arms around my body, a chill traveling across my shoulders and all the way down my arms. It had been more than a year since Thomas had died, and I was starting to wonder if that visceral reaction to his name would ever go away.

"Just to be clear, your attendance is expected at this dance," Mr. Hathaway continued. "I believe it will engender school spirit and strengthen our sense of community. If, for some reason, you are unable to attend, I expect to personally receive your excuse in writing and signed by your parents. That's how we'll be doing things around here from now on, people. Trust is a big thing with me. I'll do whatever I can to earn yours, and I hope you'll do the same for me."

Right. Making us bring an excuse note to get out of a dance was very trusting.

As Headmaster Hathaway continued to wax on about our bright new future, I glanced over my shoulder, trying to get a glimpse of Noelle. Maybe Double H would erode her earlier nonchalance and inspire her to help me bring Billings back. But as I turned, my gaze fell on someone else. Someone so distracting I forgot what I'd been thinking two seconds before.

Josh Hollis. Josh, who was no longer my Josh, but Ivy Slade's Josh. He was sitting in the back row of the boys' section, wearing a black cashmere sweater over a white T-shirt, his curly, dark blond hair slightly unruly. He seemed tense; his hands were tucked under his arms and he was pressed so far back in the pew that it looked like he was trying to fuse his spine to the wood. I saw him glance toward the aisle and followed his gaze. There sat Graham Hathaway—the usually jovial, devil-may-care Graham Hathaway—bent forward with his elbows braced on his knees, his feet bouncing beneath him, his jaw and fists clenched tightly, like he wanted to punch someone.

My eyes darted back to Josh. He was now chewing on the side of his thumb and sliding his eyes toward the exit, as if he wanted to escape.

Graham, Josh. Josh, Graham.

Did those two know each other?

The moment Mr. Hathaway dismissed us, Josh was out the side door, shoving it open with the heel of his hand. As everyone else got up and gathered their things, the room exploding with conversation, I saw Ivy look around for him. Our eyes met and I shrugged.

Never a dull moment at Easton.

TYPICAL EASTON

"Hey, Reed!" Ivy fell into step with me as everyone crowded toward the doors at the back of the chapel. "Some speech, huh? He's like the anti-Crom."

"Seriously."

We walked out into the cold, gray morning, stepping out of the way as groups of students broke off in all directions, hustling their way to class. Ivy paused, her dark eyes glinting with mischief.

"Whoa. Who's the brand-new hotness?" she asked, lifting her angular chin.

I followed her gaze. Sawyer and Graham were standing a few yards off from the chapel doors, arguing in low tones. They *were* pretty cute—Sawyer all blond and innocent, Graham with his dark hair and square jaw—all of it more intense as they went toe-to-toe. I felt a weird, proprietary twinge over Ivy thinking they were cute. Like I saw them first. Not that I was interested or anything. I had Upton. Sort of.

Still, if her reaction was any indication, the Hathaway boys were going to be cleaning up around Easton when it came to girls.

"That's Sawyer and Graham Hathaway," I said.

"Hathaway? As in . . . ?" she said, tugging her black fedora over her dark hair.

"Yep," I said. "The headmaster's sons."

"Okay. That makes them even hotter." Ivy linked her arms with mine. "Introduce me!"

An anticipatory excitement started to build in my chest. Ivy was unusually psyched to meet the new guys. Did this mean there was trouble between her and Josh? Was she scoping out a new boyfriend?

"Your wish is my command," I said with a smile.

The moment the brothers saw us approaching, they stepped slightly away from each other and both gave us a strained smile.

"Hey!" I said. I hugged Graham first, then Sawyer. He held me a tad longer than his brother did, but then, we were closer friends. "Graham, Sawyer, this is my friend Ivy Slade."

"Hi!" Ivy said, lifting a leather-gloved hand. "Welcome to our insane asylum."

The guys laughed. "Thanks," Sawyer said.

"Nice to be here," Graham added.

"So, what do you guys think of Easton?" I asked.

"It seems cool." Graham glanced around in a distracted way. His pea coat was open, even in all the crisp frigidity of January in New England, exposing the preppy sweater underneath. Before now I'd mostly seen him half dressed for the beach, so he looked to me like a little kid playing dress-up in his daddy's clothes.

"I'm sorry about Billings, Reed," Sawyer said. "I know it meant a lot to you."

"Boo-freaking-hoo!" a junior guy I barely recognized commented as he passed us, earning a round of laughter and high fives from his friends.

My face burned and I lifted a shoulder. "I guess not everyone's too upset about it." I tugged my history text and notebook out of my bag, and Ivy and I walked between the guys, heading for class. The cold wind had bitten my ears raw, so I used my free hand to pull the sides of my hat down over them. "At least we had a little bit of warning, thanks to you."

"What do you mean?" Ivy asked, shoving her hands in her pockets. "I thought no one knew about it."

"When we were down in St. Barths, Sawyer overheard a conversation between his dad, Noelle's father, and a mystery person on speakerphone," I explained.

"We knew there was *something* going on with Billings . . ." Sawyer said.

"But I thought that the administration was just talking about splitting us up or something," I added. "Not—"

"Tearing the entire thing down?" Ivy said.

"Exactly," I replied, my heart heavy.

No one could have prepared me for the sight of those bulldozers leveling Billings House, for the realization that the room I'd lived in for a year and a half had been obliterated. We'd partied and laughed and cried in those rooms. I'd been initiated there; Cheyenne Martin had died there. So many famous and powerful and influential women had studied and lived and loved in Billings House. Now, all of it was gone. With no ceremony, no fanfare, no good-byes. It was so very wrong.

"Was it your father's idea, tearing down Billings?" I asked the guys, trying not to let too much accusation seep into my voice.

Sawyer and Graham exchanged a look over our heads. "He hasn't said that—not exactly—but . . ."

"But you think it was," I finished, my fingers curling around the spines of my books.

"Don't hate him, Reed," Graham said, tossing his brown bangs off his face. "This is what he does. He goes into a school, finds the problems, and deals with them. It's all action, action, action with him. It's just the way he's wired."

"Billings wasn't a problem. And he could have given us a chance to plead our case," I said, hugging my books to my chest. "Back there he was all about an open-door policy and wanting to know what we want, but he didn't think of that before he tore down our house."

Graham paused at the foot of the steps to the class building and laughed. "It was just a dorm."

A sophomore in a pink tasseled hat pushed past us, throwing an irritated look at Graham for blocking the stairs. I pressed my lips together to keep from snapping and took a breath of the cold, dry air. "No, it wasn't. It was my home."

It was hard to express what Billings had meant to me. When

I'd first come to Easton, my family had been in shambles, and the Billings Girls had filled a serious void. They had become like sisters. Last year, even as they were testing me, they were always there when I needed them. Walking into that house had felt more comforting than walking into my home in Croton. But I couldn't expect Graham to understand that.

Sawyer leveled his brother with a glare. I could tell he wanted Graham to back off and I felt a rush of gratitude. A group of girls laughed loudly as they tromped across the frozen grass toward the class building.

"I'm sorry," Graham said, slipping one hand into his coat pocket. "I didn't know it meant so much to you."

"Well, it did," Sawyer said, his tone serious.

"Even if none of us really understood it," Ivy added lightly.

I tried not to cringe. Neither Ivy nor Josh had ever really *tried* to understand it. But then, I had to admit, they both had their reasons for hating Billings.

"Look, I know my dad can be kind of full-steam-ahead sometimes, but honestly, it's because he cares. It's not just a party line. He just wants what's best for everyone," Graham said earnestly. His eyes flicked left as a pair of teachers walked by us, clutching steaming Coffee Carma cups. He rolled his shoulders back as if he didn't want the authority figures to catch him slouching.

"And he wants to keep you safe," Sawyer added. He blew into his hands and rubbed them together. "You have to appreciate that."

I sighed, my breath making a huge steam cloud between us. "I guess when you look at it from an outsider's point of view, Billings did kind of put my life on the line more than once."

"You don't see it that way?" Ivy asked, incredulous.

"Billings wasn't the problem," I said with a sad smile. My gaze drifted reluctantly toward the empty space where the dorm had once stood. "It was the one thing that kept me going."

Graham sighed and off into the distance for a moment. I turned and saw that he was watching his dad, who stood at the center of campus, engaged in animated conversation with a group of freshman guys.

Sawyer started up the steps of the class building. "I don't know what good it'll do, but if you want me to talk to him, I will."

I was about to thank him profusely, when Ivy interrupted me.

"Josh!" she shouted. "Wait up!"

She gave us an apologetic smile.

"Sorry, guys. I gotta go."

With that, she jogged over to Josh, who had paused under a leafless oak tree to wait for her. Josh looked past Ivy at Graham, and for a moment, the two of them went completely ashen. Then Ivy threw her arms around Josh's neck and they kissed. A lot. Without coming up for air.

Great. Now I was ashen too.

Why couldn't Upton have been three years younger? And a student at Easton? And *here*? If he were here, I was sure I wouldn't be so jealous of Ivy. I was sure I wouldn't be having all these old and intense feelings for Josh. At the very least, I would have someone to smother with kisses when I started to turn green with envy.

"Graham. Don't," Sawyer said.

Graham's eyes flicked to his brother. "Don't what?" he asked tersely.

"Just don't."

Graham clenched his teeth and bowed his head forward, as if he was trying to keep himself from exploding.

"I have to get out of here," he muttered.

Then he turned and stormed off in the opposite direction from where Ivy and Josh stood.

"Do you guys know Josh Hollis?" I asked Sawyer. "Back at the chapel it looked like Graham wanted to hit someone, and I'm thinking it was Josh."

Sawyer took a deep breath. His face was growing red from his chin up to his forehead, whether from the cold or something else, I couldn't tell.

"It's a long story," he said, starting after his brother. He walked backward for a second to look at me. "I'll explain later."

"Wait! What about class?" I called after him as he jogged to catch up with Graham, his one-shouldered backpack bouncing behind him.

"Being the son of the headmaster has its perks!" he shouted back.

I watched them until my eyes started to sting from the cold. When I glanced back at the tree again, Josh and Ivy were gone.

You don't need him anymore, Reed. You have Upton, remember? We had decided to not put labels on our relationship—to simply stay in touch—so maybe that was what I should be doing right now.

I whipped out my phone and texted my casual European boy toy.

How many days till I graduate?

He responded as I was climbing the steps into the class building.

Unclear. Will do the math & respond ASAP. BTW, what are you wearing? :)

I rolled my eyes with a laugh and shoved my phone back in my bag without replying. But at least I wasn't thinking about Josh and Ivy anymore. Really. Not at all.

THE BILLINGS LITERARY SOCIETY

"At least we're living in the same dorm," Constance said, skipping for a few steps as we walked across campus toward Pemberly that night. Her red curls bounced around her shoulders and her cherubic cheeks were pink from the cold. "Hey! Maybe you can switch with Lorna! Give her your single so we can room together again!"

I pondered this idea for a moment, but not very seriously. "I don't know. I kind of like my solitude."

And as much as I loved Constance, I wasn't sure I could deal with her nonstop talking 24/7. I didn't think our friendship could survive it.

"Oh. Okay. Well, that's cool. You're only two floors away anyway," Constance said with a shrug.

"Yep. Just two floors."

I wished I could be as enthusiastic as she was, but I couldn't. It was only the first day of school and I was already loaded down with library books for my new history paper. Plus my right foot was frozen solid after stepping in a slush puddle outside the dining hall. And to top it all off, I had spent the day promising my friends that I was going to figure out a way to bring back Billings, yet I felt less and less certain every time I uttered the words.

Where could I even begin? Should I talk to Hathaway? Petition the board? Hold a fund-raiser to show them we were committed to rebuilding? And even if any of that worked, and they decided to build a new Billings on the old site, it wouldn't really be Billings. Not our Billings, with all its history. Plus there was no way it would be finished before the seniors graduated in June, so Noelle, Tiff, Portia, Rose, Shelby, London, and Vienna were out of luck no matter how you looked at it.

"Oh! Reed! Don't look!" Constance whispered, stopping suddenly and slapping her gloved hand over my eyes.

"Constance! What the heck are you doing?" I said with a laugh, batting her hand away.

That was when my pity party hit an all-time roar. Because Ivy and Josh were standing just outside the door to our dorm, making out again, this time in the dim glow of the overhead lights. God. Hadn't these two ever heard the phrase "get a room"? I glanced at Constance, my eyes desperate. As if reading my thoughts, she turned and walked purposely forward.

"Hi, guys!" she said brightly.

They sprang apart, snagged.

"Hey!" Ivy said, her face happily flushed. "Sorry. You guys probably want to get inside."

Constance shot me a mothering look that made me want to cry for all my patheticness.

"No worries," I said, angling to get by them.

"Reed, how are you?" Josh asked, clearing his throat and shoving his hands into the pockets of his heather gray coat. His lips were red and puffy from all the face-sucking. Fab.

"Great. Fine. You?" I asked.

You have Upton. Beautiful, worldly Upton. Stop wanting to rip Josh away from Ivy.

"Great," he replied.

Upton, Upton, Upton.

"Great."

Can I go inside now and eat an entire carton of coffee ice cream?

"I'm good, too!" Constance announced helpfully.

"Right. Yeah. Sorry, Constance." Josh scratched the back of his neck. "I guess I should go."

"Yeah. I should get inside before I freeze," Ivy said, giving Josh a quick kiss. "Call you later?"

"Definitely," he replied. "Bye, Reed. Constance."

He lifted a hand, but I was already through the door.

"Later!" Constance said loudly.

I was definitely calling Upton the second I got upstairs.

Constance and I walked up the stairs to the second floor with Ivy trailing slightly behind. Constance kept shooting me these concerned looks out the corner of her eye and I prayed she wouldn't say anything embarrassing in front of Ivy.

"Well. This is me," Constance said as we arrived at her floor. "You guys want to come hang out? Lorna's probably over at Missy's. As always."

"Thanks, Constance, but I really have to get to work on this paper," I said, trying to thank her silently for helping me out downstairs.

"And I just want to pass out," Ivy added, catching up with us. "But thanks. Maybe some other time."

"Okay. 'Night!" Constance smiled and whipped around, her red hair flying, leaving me and Ivy entirely alone. We shared a somewhat awkward smile and then walked side by side up the stairs to our adjacent rooms.

Ivy's steps were slow, her breathing labored, and I realized with a pang that she was still recovering from the gunshot. The one that Sabine had intended for me, but had ended up hitting her when Josh had grabbed for the gun in Sabine's hand. Ivy *looked* healthy, though. Her ivory skin was flawless, her thick black hair shiny and coiffed, her body still slim. She had seemed fine that morning, but maybe a full day of activity had worn her out. She winced as we reached the third-floor landing, clearly in pain.

All thanks to me. And Josh. And the fact that Josh had risked his own life to save me. Because he loved me. He'd told me as much when Ivy was in the hospital, but he hadn't wanted to leave her then, and I hadn't wanted him to, either. Ivy was my friend, and she needed Josh right then. End of story.

But the question was, did Josh *still* love me? If all the tongue-on-tongue sessions those two were having today were any indication, he did not. It seemed like something had changed while I'd been down in St. Barths. Josh and Ivy were definitely in deep now.

I sighed, longing for Upton all over again. But did I really want him, or did I just want to prove to Josh and Ivy that I'd moved on, too?

"So, how was your break?" I asked. *Please don't tell me you spent the entire time fooling around with Josh.*

"It was good," Ivy said. "I actually hung out a lot with my friends from last year—from my school in Boston? It was cool to see them again."

"Yeah? What are they like?" I asked, glad the conversation was shifting away from our mutual love.

Ivy laughed. "They're . . . fun. You'd like them. We kind of tear it up when we get together. Not that I could do much while I was recovering, but it was cool."

"What do you mean, 'tear it up'?" I asked as we arrived at our floor. I pushed the stairwell door open and we stepped into the hall.

She lifted a shoulder. "They're big into the music scene and a lot of them are skate- or snowboarders, so with them it's all about going to clubs and staying out all night and daring each other to do insane things. They actually built a skate park on the roof of my house the last night we were home. I still can't believe my dad let them do that," she said with a fond laugh.

"Wow. Sounds like fun," I said. And very different from the Easton crowd.

"Yeah. They're cool," she said wistfully. "I always thought I'd have a group like that at Easton, but I never really jelled with anyone here that way." Then she focused on me and blushed. "I mean, until recently."

"Nice save," I joked.

Ivy smiled. "So . . . are you okay?" she asked as she removed the white hood from over her jet-black hair. "You know I wasn't a huge Billings fan, but—"

"I'm fine," I replied. "Just exhausted. It's been a long day."

"Yeah, and it looks like Mr. Barber is jumping right back in," she said, eyeing my history-related library books. We paused outside the doors to our rooms. I could hear her roommate, Jillian Crane, inside, singing along to the latest movie musical sound track. Ivy rolled her eyes. "There's no accounting for her taste in music."

"Seriously," I replied with a laugh.

"Want to come in and help me gag her?" Ivy asked, tilting her head toward the door.

"That's okay," I said, lifting the books. "I think I'm just going to make some notes on these and go to sleep."

"Okay. Well, if you need coffee or anything, my mom got me one of those pod things for Christmas, so I'm all over it."

"Thanks," I replied, my heart giving a tug. Ivy was great, but it was kind of tough being friends with the person who was smooching my boyfriend all over campus.

Ahem, *ex*-boyfriend.

"'Night," she said.

"'Night."

I slipped into my room, closed the door, and sighed. Then

something caught my eye in the dim light streaming through the slim window from the quad. I froze and my vision went fuzzy with fear. I blinked and shook my head, but it was still there. Lying in the center of my bed was a package, about the size and shape of a hardcover novel, wrapped in plain brown paper. Instantly, memories of blush beads and black balls and perfume bottles and Cheyenne Martin's clothing crowded my brain. Dozens of sadistic gifts and e-mails left for me to find. Left for me to fear.

Who had put this in my room? And why? Was Sabine back? Could she possibly, somehow, be back? But no. She was in jail somewhere. Awaiting trial. Locked up all safe and sound.

I flipped on the lights. Dropped the books on my shabby wood desk. Stood over the package.

Don't open it. Just throw it out. This is the last thing you need.

The edge of a cream-colored envelope stuck out from beneath the package. There was some kind of swirling design stamped on it in thick brown ink. I carefully tugged the note card out as if the package might explode if I made the wrong move. The design was a three-pointed crest, filled with swirling roses. At the top of the middle point were a quill and a hammer, crossed like swords. In the very center of the crest were three letters entwined together in an elaborate script.

B. L. S.

Okay. Now I was intrigued. Against my better judgment, I opened the envelope. The card inside read simply, *For Reed Brennan, Given with trust and pride. Your sisters in BLS.*

Sisters in what now? I glanced at the package. Trust and pride.

That didn't seem scary at all. I sat down on the bed and cautiously picked up the hefty package. Popping the first piece of tape didn't result in an explosion of shrapnel, so I tore the rest of it open. Inside was an old, worn, leather-bound book with the BLS crest etched into the cover. Carefully, I opened the book. Its spine creaked with age. The pages were heavy yellow parchment, brown and ragged at the edges. The words on the first page were handwritten in gorgeous black script.

The Billings Literary Society. Founded December 3, A.D. 1915.

For a long moment I couldn't move. Then I looked around at the four blank, off-white walls of my room as if someone was going to be sitting there, waiting to pounce. Satisfied that I was alone, I slowly turned the page, touching only the very corner, not wanting to mar what was obviously a very old and precious book. On the second page, handwritten again, was a creed.

We, the undersigned, do hereby pledge our hearts and minds to the purposes of the Billings Literary Society. We promise to be loyal, steadfast, and true to all who join our circle. We vow never to reveal the secrets of our society, but to uphold its values and standards in the face of tyranny. Blood to blood, ashes to ashes, sister to sister, we make this sacred vow.

Under the creed, eleven names were signed in various handwriting styles, some loopy and large, some tiny and tight—all perfectly legible. My eyes scanned the names. Jane Barton, Marilyn DeMeers, Lavender Lewis-Tarrington, Catherine White, Elizabeth Williams, Theresa Billings.

Theresa Billings? As in *Billings* Billings?

I checked the date at the bottom of the list. It had been signed on December 3, 1915.

A door slammed in the hallway and my heart all but stopped. I took a breath, my eyes snagging on the plastic basket full of shower supplies on top of my dresser. Had this dorm even been here back then?

Probably not. In 1915, Easton Academy had been an all boys' school. The Billings School for Girls had been established just up the road, and the two facilities had been kind of like sister/brother schools, one grooming boys to be captains of industry, leaders of the free world, and artists, musicians, or authors; the other grooming girls to be their wives. Back in the 1970s, Easton had absorbed the Billings students and Billings had been shut down. As far as I knew, Billings House had been named by the Easton administration as their nod to the old girls' school.

In 1915, Billings School for Girls had been a functioning academy for the daughters of the elite. But what was the Billings Literary Society? Who had left this precious book for me and why?

Instantly I thought of Susan Llewellyn, the Billings alumni I knew better than any other—and also one of the coolest women on earth. Suzel had helped us out last semester when we'd been banned from leaving the campus for the Legacy—the most exclusive party of the year—by showing us a secret tunnel that led from campus to the outside world. Obviously whoever put this book in my room had to be a Billings alum. Was Suzel trying to pass on this bit of the Billings legacy now that it appeared the house was gone for good?

I quickly turned the page and was greeted by the words *Requirements for Admission into the Society*.

The list included qualities such as "intelligence," "progressive thinking," "eloquence," "industry," and "loyalty." Apparently the members talked about literature as well as current events, poetry, science, religion, and all kinds of things. But above all, they were friends. Loyal, steadfast, and true.

"Oh my God," I whispered as I finished paging through the first half of the book and realized with a jolt exactly what the Billings Literary Society was: a progressive, secret club for hardworking, forward-thinking women, disguised as a literary group.

My thoughts instantly turned to Ivy. She'd looked so wistful when she'd mentioned that she'd never found a true group of friends at Easton. Ivy would love the language, the camaraderie, the very idea of swearing loyalty to a group of girls who wanted nothing more than to be themselves—to learn what they wanted to learn rather than what their teachers decided they should.

The whole thing was so incredibly cool.

I took a deep breath and kept reading. The book outlined three specific group tasks that each girl would have to participate in and pass in order to qualify for membership in the sisterhood. The first would prove the prospective member's intelligence by requiring her to answer five questions on the history of Billings within a finite space of time. The book described holding a candle at an angle over the potential sister's hand and making her answer before the hot wax dripped over her skin.

Kind of fishy, but these ancient secret organizations were into that kind of stuff, right?

The second task tested her loyalty by playing a game in which the potentials were rewarded for saying positive things about one another, and penalized for saying anything negative. The third task involved "working together to beautify or improve some particular aspect of our school." During each of these tasks, the potentials would be observed by their "pledge mistress" and evaluated for membership based on their performance.

I smiled to myself. I'd never been involved in vetting Easton students for invitations into Billings House, but from what I'd heard and experienced, getting in had been more of a matter of proving your ability to take a dare than proving your work ethic.

I turned the page and found an entire section on initiation, complete with intricate drawings of white robes, black and white candles, and formations delineating where each member and initiate should stand during the ceremony. My heart gave a flutter at the beautifully rendered portraits of the girls in black, facing the girls in white. It looked almost exactly the way our initiations had looked. Some of this ritual had clearly trickled down to the current—well, former—Billings House.

Suddenly, I felt like part of something big—bigger than I'd ever truly realized.

These first few chapters of text had all been written in the same hand. I flipped to the original list of signatures to compare the hand-writing and concluded that Elizabeth Williams had been the mastermind behind the Billings Literary Society. All the rituals and tasks had been written out in her tight script. I felt like she was reading over my shoulder, urging me on, encouraging me to keep reading. So I did.

With each new page, my heart beat faster and faster. There was a secret handshake. A secret whistle. A whispered question and answer to recite before admission into secret meetings. There was even a list of excuses to recite should a faculty member happen to stumble upon one of said meetings. I raced ahead, speed-reading and skimming, my smile widening slowly.

This was it.

This was the key to bringing the Billings Girls back together—and maybe even getting Ivy the circle of friends she'd always wanted. A secret society. The Billings Literary Society, to be exact. We could reconstitute it. We could reclaim our history. We could be the sort of society the original Billings Girls wanted us to be. Forget adherence to fashion codes and backbiting gossip and snarky texts. We could be the fine, upstanding, intelligent, world-leading women of tomorrow.

With a secret handshake and everything.

I slammed the book closed and hopped off my bed. Noelle had to see this ASAP. If this book didn't awaken her inner Billings Girl, nothing would.

ULTIMATE BILLINGS GIRL

"They cover everything in here, Noelle." I dropped down on the bed next to her, so hard we both bounced.

Noelle's Pemberly single was just two floors above mine and completely barren. She hadn't hung up any of the framed photographs of her family and friends, or the black-and-white reproductions of classic *Vogue* covers that had lined the walls in her Billings room. Usually her desk and dresser were covered with crap—scarves, necklaces, iPods, books, ticket stubs, flyers, makeup, mementos—but she hadn't unpacked a thing other than the clothes and makeup she'd worn that day.

I hugged the book to my chest like it was the Holy Grail. "Initiation rites, mission statements, proper conduct when meeting with a sister in public. It's a guidebook *and* a diary of everything these girls ever did. There are entries dating all the way up until the 1970s!"

"It *is* an intriguing little piece of history," Noelle said, giving a cursory glance over my shoulder. "Let me see that list of original members again."

I handed her the book, open to the second page. She quickly scanned the names. For a moment I saw her pause and her lips flicked into a smile, but then her eyes narrowed and the smile was gone.

"What? Do you recognize a name?" I asked.

Noelle slapped the book closed and handed it back to me. "Nope."

She got up and walked over to her trunk, unsnapping the lid and throwing it open. In big armfuls, she started to remove her clothes, most of them already on hangers, and shoved them into her teeny closet at random. Silk blouses shimmied to the floor. Designer dresses crowded and wrinkled. She tossed a stack of three-hundred-dollar jeans on the shelf above the hanging rod; four pairs tumbled back down onto her head. She groaned and flung them onto the floor.

"What's the matter?" I asked.

"Nothing," she told the pile of jeans.

"Noelle—"

"Why would someone give that to you?" Noelle blurted, throwing a hand out at me.

"Because. Clearly they want us to restart this Billings Literary Society thing, and I—"

Noelle closed her eyes, shook her head, and let out that condescending laugh of hers that always got right under my skin. "No. No. Why would someone give it to *you*?"

Oh. I got it. She wanted the book. She thought I didn't deserve to have it and she did. I felt a flash of anger and clutched the book tighter. "What am I, not Billings Girl enough for you?"

So maybe I had been voted out of the house before Christmas break, but that had been personal—because I'd hooked up with her ex (at the time) Dash McCafferty. And we'd since learned that both of us had been drugged to within an inch of our lives by Sabine, so it wasn't entirely our fault. Not to mention the fact that Noelle had already gotten back together with Dash and asked me to move back into Billings, which I'd be doing right now if it wasn't leveled.

Noelle rolled her eyes. "No! It's not that. It's just—" She turned toward the closet again and brought her hand to her forehead. I'd never seen her this worked up. This was not the reaction I'd been expecting. "Forget it. It's nothing."

"Maybe . . . I don't know . . . maybe they left it for me because I was the last elected president of Billings," I said with a shrug. "These pages seem to be all about following rules and codes and laws. . . . Maybe whoever left it for me takes that kind of thing seriously."

"Whatever," Noelle said, bending to pick up the jeans. "I don't care."

I smiled. "Good! Because I think we should get started right away. There are all these supplies to get and we'll probably have to set up a secret email account for—"

Noelle turned around to face me. "No. I mean, I don't care," she said firmly. "I'm not doing this."

I paused as I flipped through the pages, holding the edge of one thick sheet. "Not doing what?"

"This secret society thing," she said with a trace of a sneer. She yanked a few scarves from her trunk and tossed them onto the hooks in her closet.

"You're kidding," I said as she jammed a bevy of belts onto the hooks over the scarves.

"Do I look like I'm kidding?" she asked, overturning her makeup bag atop her dresser. Tubes of mascara and eyeliner rolled in all directions and she scrambled to grab them before they hit the floor. "Is this entire dorm crooked?" she snapped, jamming her things back into the bag.

"Noelle. Come on," I said. "This could be so cool. And it's the perfect way to keep us all together. I mean, you were right this morning. It was crazy to think I could bring back Billings House, but maybe we can bring back the Billings *Girls*."

"Not interested," Noelle replied. Like she was turning down the last blueberry muffin at breakfast, rather than rejecting me and all of our friends in two short words. My blood boiled and I slammed the book closed just to keep from exploding.

"What do you mean, 'not interested'?" I demanded. "Look, I know this could be a lot of work, but we need this, Noelle. We have to keep the Billings Girls together."

"Why?" Noelle asked, her arms wide as she turned to me again. "Why do I have to do anything anymore?"

My face fell. This defeated, questioning, pleading person was not the Noelle I knew. I felt like I'd just been told all over again that there was no Santa Claus. That Elmo was just a puppet. That reality TV was not, in actuality, real.

Noelle leaned back against the wall next to the closet and shook her head, staring off into space. For the first time I noticed that there were dark circles under her eyes—that her hair wasn't perfectly parted and smooth, but unkempt and shoved haphazardly behind her ears. She slid down the wall slightly, so that her feet were pressed into the floor and her legs at a forty-five-degree angle—like she was trying to hold the wall up with her back. I'd never seen Noelle appear so spent.

"I'm not even supposed to be here," she said quietly. "I should be starting my second semester at Yale, not doing time in freaking Pemberly."

"I know," I said, my heart and chest full.

"I didn't get to finish my senior year when I should have, all because I made some seriously stupid choices," she said.

I breathed in and out slowly, trying not to imagine Thomas tied up in the woods somewhere. Trying not to think about Ariana's ice blue eyes as she threatened to throw me off the Billings roof. That was all over. This—this book I was holding—this was my future.

"So I need to make another choice now," Noelle said, pushing herself away from the wall. "And my choice is to keep my head down and my nose clean, and graduate. End of story."

I swallowed hard, my eyes stinging with tears. A few days ago, while we were still in St. Barths, we'd decided to room together in Billings. I'd had all these fantasies of staying up late and chatting all night long, being together like real sisters. Now, not only could that dream never come true, but she was completely blowing me off.

"Noelle, come on," I said, hugging the book to my chest. "I can't do this without you. Billings isn't Billings without you."

She glanced ruefully at the book. "Apparently, someone out there thinks it is."

All at once, the anger bubbled up again. Was she really going to be that petty? Noelle Lange, ultimate Billings Girl, was going to let all her sisters down just because some ancient alumna had chosen me over her?

"Who cares? This isn't about them, it's about us."

"Reed, enough already, you're giving me a headache," Noelle said, squeezing her eyes shut.

I snorted a laugh. "Fine. Forget it. I'll just do it alone."

"Good luck," she said sarcastically.

"Thanks a lot," I shot back.

On my way out, I made sure to slam the door hard enough to send those hastily folded jeans sprawling back onto her head.

PARTNER

I was up all night reading through The Book, as I had come to call it in my mind. Capital T, capital B. By Tuesday morning I was exhausted and hooked. I sat on my unmade bed, rereading Elizabeth's diary-style entries about the vetting and initiation of the first members of the society. This was where she started to mention Catherine White all over the place.

Catherine and I spent the afternoon evaluating the new class of girls for membership in the society. . . . Catherine and I wrote to the proprietor of the general store in town and have secured the necessary supplies for our initiation tomorrow night. . . . We are both filled with trepidation at the thought of the path we have chosen, but we are confident as well, knowing that wherever it may lead, we will travel it together.

Clearly, Elizabeth had a partner. A friend. Someone helping her with every aspect of getting the BLS started.

I sat up straight. Just like Elizabeth had her Catherine, I needed someone to travel the path with. Someone who would find this whole thing as intriguing as I did. Noelle wouldn't help me, but she wasn't my only friend.

I considered the other senior Billings Girls. Rose had always been obsessed with the rituals of Billings, but she could be meek and wishy-washy. Tiffany was loyal, but she'd made a deal with her dad to work in his studio in New York on the weekends, so she wasn't going to be around much, and when she was she'd be busy catching up on work. London wouldn't do it without Vienna and vice versa. So that left Portia and Shelby. Not exactly trailblazing types.

Lorna and Missy were out because they were practically my sworn enemies. Astrid and Kiki were both cool, but independent and busy—not exactly sidekick types. Which left Constance.

Constance was a good friend. There was no denying it. Loyal, steadfast, and true? You bet. But when it came to taking chances, to being brave, to breaking rules, she was not in the top five—not even the top ten—Billings Girls. Plus she was a babbler, no doubt about it. And she was dating Walt Whittaker, whose grandmother was on the board of directors. If she told him anything and he told Grandma, I'd be in deep trouble. Because, really, what was a secret society if not a social club—exactly the sort of club Double H had outlawed in his opening speech?

No. Whomever I asked to work with me on the BLS was going to have to be fearless, creative, strong, and an expert secret-keeper.

Suddenly, Ivy's favorite alt-rock band started screaming through the wall right next to my head. I laughed and glanced at the clock. Guess that was my official wake-up call. I swung my legs over the side of the bed and paused. An excited thrill shot right through me.

Ivy. Why not Ivy?

Ivy had been there for me when no one else had. She'd helped me figure out that it was Sabine who'd been stalking me, when everyone else—including almost all of the Billings Girls—had written me off as a backstabbing loser.

The door of Ivy's room opened and slammed—Jillian leaving for her thrice-weekly, crack-of-dawn yoga group in the gym. I slipped out of my room, my heart jumping around erratically as if I were jacked up on ten cups of black coffee. I knocked on Ivy's door hard, making sure she could hear me over the music. She threw the door open, half dressed in a white tank top and black wide-leg pants, her dark hair hanging over her eyes.

"Do not tell me to turn down the music!" she shouted. "I barely slept last night and I need it. It's my caffeine."

"I don't care about the music!" I shouted back, shutting the door behind me. I walked into her room, made cozy by a ton of throw pillows and colorful scarves that were tacked to the ceiling to hide the ugly stucco. "I have two words for you: Secret society."

Her eyes narrowed even further. Then she turned and walked over to her iPod dock on her desk, dousing the music. "I'm sorry. I couldn't hear you. I thought you just said 'secret society.'"

"I did." I placed the book on her desk next to her laptop, directly within her vision. She tilted her head, intrigued.

"What's this?" She ran her fingertips over the crest etched into the cover.

"It's kind of like a rule book, that was written in 1915," I told her, the excitement evident in my voice. "By the original members of the Billings Literary Society."

Ivy's fingers recoiled, as if the seal had shocked her. "Billings? You can't be serious."

"Ivy, come on. Just hear me out."

She shoved her thick hair off her face and turned away from me, red blotches appearing on her milky cheeks. Storming over to her closet as best she could in the tiny room, she yanked a gray wool sweater off a hanger, as if every move she made were an exclamation point.

"Let's just do a little recap, shall we? When I was a Billings pledge, the sisters made me break into my grandmother's house as a prank, which resulted in my grandma having a full-on stroke that eventually killed her," Ivy said, whipping a black sweater down from the shelf and comparing it to the gray one. "I don't want to have anything to do with Billings."

"But Ivy, this is different," I said, picking up the book and hugging it. "This book explains what the original Billings Girls were all about. It talks about integrity, intelligence, activism. . . . Come on. Please just look at it? It's amazing."

Ivy turned around and eyed the book. "Shouldn't you be consulting the great and mighty Noelle Lange about this?" she said sarcastically. "Last time I checked, I wasn't even *in* Billings."

"Noelle shot me down," I said, knowing that Ivy would be more likely to work with me if Noelle was not going to be involved. She did, in fact, look up at me, her eyes wide with interest. "And besides, you were *supposed* to be in Billings. They invited you. You turned *them* down." I walked over to her. "Look, someone left this book for me. An alumna or someone. Which means they're trusting me to start this thing up again. Me. My decisions. And I want to include you. If this was 1915, believe me, you'd fit every one of their qualifications."

Ivy narrowed her eyes, letting her hands, which were still clutching the sweaters, fall at her sides. "Fine. Let me see it."

Before I could even hand it over, she quickly dropped the clothes, snatched the book, and sat down on her bed with it. She flipped through the first few pages, but then gradually slowed down, taking in the words. I could just feel it washing over her. The ancient handwriting, the musty leather scent, the sophisticated language. It was getting to her, just like it had gotten to me. I saw her pause on the creed, reading it over again and again. She skimmed over the tasks and the initiation, but took some time reading over Elizabeth's diary entries. When she smiled, I smiled. This was working. It was totally working.

Finally she flipped back to the beginning and eyed the eleven signatures for a long moment. She frowned with interest, then slapped the book closed and folded her arms over the cover.

"Okay," she said, looking up at me. "I'll do it."

I grinned, my heart leaping in my chest. "Just like that?"

"Nope. On one condition," Ivy said. She stood up and held the book in both hands.

I blinked. Why did I not like the sound of this? "What condition?"

"We have to do everything exactly the way the book says," Ivy told me, laying her hand flat atop the BLS seal. "Follow every rule, every detail, down to the letter."

"But you haven't even read the whole thing," I protested, thinking of the entry about the Billings Literary Society and its *eleven* members. Billings already had fourteen members, including me and Noelle. Even if Noelle was truly out, we'd have too many girls. Especially with Ivy involved. Plus I'd been thinking about opening it up to some of our other friends. Ivy's roommate, Jillian; my friend Diana Waters . . . people who might have made it into Billings next year—if it had still been around.

"Doesn't matter," she said, shaking her head. "If we're going to do this right, we have to honor the original Billings Girls," Ivy said, cautiously opening the book to the page about the requirements for sisterhood. "These girls were insanely cool, do you realize that?"

"Uh, yeah!" I said, tucking my long brown hair behind my ear. "That's why I knew you'd be in."

"And they were also clearly *way* ahead of their time," Ivy continued. "This is their legacy. We can't screw with it. Otherwise, what's the point?" She offered her hand.

"Well? What do you say? Is it a deal?"

I held my breath. We could talk about membership numbers later. Right now, all I wanted to do was get started. "Deal."

She put the book down on her bed and we shook on it, both of us grinning.

"Just one question," she said, turning to grab the gray sweater up off the floor. "Why me?"

I thought about saying I wanted to help her find that elusive group of Easton friends she'd been looking for, but she would have tossed me out on my butt for pitying her. Besides, that wasn't the only reason. I lifted my shoulders. "I trust you."

"Yeah?" she asked as she yanked the sweater over her head.

"Is that such a shock? You helped me figure out who was stalking me," I reminded her. "You basically took a bullet for me. How could I not trust you?"

Ivy laughed. "I take a bullet for you and all I get is a dusty book?"

"You get a whole secret society. With a secret whistle and everything," I said.

And the love of my life, I thought to myself as Ivy tore through the pages. *But who's counting?*

GHOSTS

Later that night, I sat at a wooden study carrel all the way at the back of the first-floor stacks. The library was so silent that my fingers tapping on my laptop's keyboard sounded like rapid-fire gunshots. Every now and then I'd hear the distant sound of a book being dragged from a shelf, or the slow flap of a page being turned, but otherwise, nothing. Apparently, on the second night back after break, people weren't all that motivated yet.

Bam!

I jumped back in my chair and nearly tumbled to the floor. Ivy slipped into the chair at the study carrel next to mine and pointed to the book, which she'd just dropped on the desk.

My hands on my chest, I gasped for breath. "God, Ivy! Are you trying to give me a heart attack?"

The gray-haired librarian padded over to the end of our aisle to give us a stern look. I shot her an apologetic grimace as Ivy dropped her bag on the floor, then opened the book. "I know where the chapel is," she said.

The librarian shuffled away again and Ivy turned to the page that outlined the procedures for society meetings. There was a gorgeous sketch of a clapboard chapel, surrounded by trees. She pointed at it and leaned in closer to my side.

"If we're going to do this right, we're going to do it there," she said. "The old Billings School chapel. It was supposed to be demolished a couple of years ago, but then some historical organization came in and stopped it. There was a big story about it in the paper my sophomore year—how they were going to renovate it—but I don't think they ever did."

She angled my computer toward her, saved my history paper, and opened my browser.

"What're you doing?" I asked.

"Showing it to you," she said, moving her finger over the touch pad.

She brought up the Easton Academy website, all blue and gold and austere, with a photo of our own chapel anchoring the front page. Under the history section, she clicked the tab titled *The Billings School for Girls*. I scooted forward, scanning the contents.

"Here." Ivy clicked on a link. "Campus map."

A line drawing of the old Billings campus popped up. There had only been a few buildings: living quarters for students and teachers; the McKinley Building, which housed classrooms, offices, and a small library; the Prescott Building, which was basically the gymnasium and dining room; and the chapel.

"This is that apartment building down the hill from the Easton entry gate," Ivy said, pointing at McKinley, the largest of the structures.

"Yeah. And isn't the Prescott Building the Easton YMCA now?" I said.

"Yep. And *that* is the old chapel . . ." Ivy said, pointing. "It's on our side of Hamilton Parkway, just up the hill from campus."

"By the clearing," I said with a shiver of recognition. The clearing was the spot where the Billings/Ketlar parties used to be held. Where Thomas and I had fought the night before he disappeared.

"Yeah, it's a short walk back from there," Ivy said. "We used to hang out there every once in a while until they had it condemned. After that, only the 'real' rebels used it," she said sarcastically. I smirked. There weren't any real rebels at Easton, just poseurs who thought they were rebels. She slapped my laptop closed and grabbed her bag. "Let's go check it out."

"What? Now? It's pitch-black out *and* it's snowing," I protested, even as I rose from my chair.

"I swiped flashlights from the supply closet and you have snow boots on. Come on!"

Ivy's excitement was infectious, and I grabbed my stuff and shoved it all into my bag. Pulling my hat down over my hair, I placed the book carefully inside my bag next to my computer and followed her out.

The snow fluttered down from the sky lazily, like millions of tiny, weightless feathers, tickling our noses as we hurried across campus. Our feet left long tracks in the snow behind us as we ignored the shoveled pathways. My heart hollowed out when we passed the huge patch of dirt where Billings used to be, the front walkway now leading to nowhere. I averted my eyes and quickened my pace. I was going to fix this. Right here, right now, I was taking my first steps toward bringing Billings back.

When we reached the very edge of campus, Ivy and I paused and looked over our shoulders. There were only a few souls out on the grounds, all of them indistinguishable in the darkness, and none of them interested in us. They were too busy huddling into their scarves and coats, rushing back to the warmth of their dorms. We still had an hour before we were technically supposed to be inside our houses, but it seemed like most people had already hunkered down for the night. Ivy and I looked at one another in anticipation, took a breath, and ran. Our feet crunched through the untouched snow on this side of campus. It was slow going, even as we tried to hurry, and soon my lungs started to burn. With every step I waited for the shout—the voice telling us to stop, come back, that we weren't allowed past the tree line. But, mercifully, it never came.

As we ducked into the woods at the top of the hill we slowed to catch our breath. The snow wasn't as deep under the trees, the leaves carrying the brunt of the burden, and we flicked the flashlights on, following the familiar path toward the clearing. My heart pounded with nerves, excitement, and sadness as we came to the clearing.

"Reed? Come on," Ivy said, urging me forward.

I hadn't even realized I'd paused.

"Yeah. Coming."

We slid over fallen leaves, ducked branches here and there, and finally came to the end of the pathway. Rising up in front of us was an old white clapboard church, the steeple collapsing in on itself, the steps that led to the double doors crumbling. Two fluorescent orange signs nailed to the doors had DANGER! CONDEMNED! stamped across them, but the two-by-fours nailed across the door had been pried free. One of the doors hung slightly ajar, creaking in the wind.

"Okay. This is spooky," I said, shivering so violently I had to hug myself to stop it.

"Spooky, but beautiful," Ivy replied, running the beam of the flashlight over the dirty white planks of wood. "Shall we?"

I swallowed my fear. This was for Billings. "Sure."

We picked our way carefully up the crumbling steps and pushed open the door. It cried out in protest, and the noise rousted some birds—or perhaps bats—from their hiding places, sending them flapping into the night sky. Inside, the chapel was bone-numbingly cold—even colder, it seemed, than the air outside. We stood in the corner of the long, rectangular room and shone our flashlights across the small space. There were several dusty pews with a wide aisle down the center facing an old altar, and half a dozen wall sconces held melted candles, their wax frozen in drips over their bases. The wood floor was littered with garbage. Cigarette butts, beer bottles, old joints, crumpled fast-food bags. The place was a sty.

"I don't really think my friends are going to like hanging out here," I said wryly, taking a few tentative steps into the room.

"My friends would *love* it," she said with a glint in her eye. "Of course, they would probably tag the crap out of it."

I chuckled as my footsteps on the chapel's aisle caused a cacophony of creaks and wails. Actually, I was surprised there had been no outright vandalism inside the chapel. Garbage aplenty, yeah, but no spray paint or anything.

"We have to use it," Ivy said. "It has the history." She edged her way along the right side of the room, down the side aisle, and peered through an open archway riddled with cobwebs. Apparently finding nothing of interest there, she kept walking toward the pulpit at the front of the chapel. "We could clean it up. Make it more livable. With all new candles lit and the wood polished up, it could be amazing."

I took a breath. The stained-glass windows were beautiful and mostly intact, only a few of them cracked here and there. With candles glowing, and maybe some pillows and cozy blankets, the ambience could be just right.

An idea suddenly hit me like a kick to the gut. The third task. I'd been wondering what sort of chore we could devise to fit the requirements of beautifying or improving some aspect of the school. This was perfect. We could clean up the old Billings chapel—the space our sisters used to gather in—and make it suitable for ourselves. It was like someone had just wrapped up a huge gift and dropped it in my lap.

I smiled up at the high ceiling. *Thanks, Elizabeth Williams.*

Ivy grinned, her face partially shadowed in the shifting light. "You're loving me now, aren't you?"

I rolled my eyes and turned for the door. "Come on. Let's get back to Pemberly. We have a lot of work to do."

I took one look back at the chapel as I stepped out, and a chill went through me. I paused, my heart in my throat, feeling like someone was watching me. Then I took a breath and shook it off. It was just the darkness, the coldness, the desertedness. Soon this place would be inhabited again, by laughter and conversation and light. Soon this place would belong to Billings again.

TAPS

"I don't understand. Why are you inviting Noelle?" Ivy asked.

She sat back against the side of my bed, holding an old-fashioned quill pen between her fingers. Laid out on the wood floor between us were several cream-colored cards and envelopes, which she had pur-chased at the Paperie—an exclusive stationer in Easton—the previous afternoon. It was 6 a.m. on Wednesday and we'd been working on the invites since four, trying to get them done before breakfast, chapel, and classes got in the way. My back was killing me from bending over the cards, but time was running out, so I just had to suck it up if we were going to mail these out this morning.

"She's a Billings Girl. I can't just not invite her to join the Billings Literary Society," I said, holding the edges of one of the stationery cards between my palms as I inspected my handwriting. Altogether we were filling out fifteen invitations. One for each Billings Girl and one for Ivy. I hadn't even mentioned the idea of inviting more people, not wanting to risk too many of my friends being cut if it really came down to that.

"But she already turned you down," Ivy replied, tossing her long dark hair back from her face. She leaned forward and carefully addressed an envelope. "Do you really want to get rejected twice?"

"Look, I know you don't like her," I began, "but I—"

"It's not because I don't like her," Ivy said, fixing me with a stare. "I mean, okay, I think she's the devil incarnate—"

I snorted a laugh. She didn't join me. Damn. She was serious.

"It's just, there are only eleven open spots," Ivy continued. "Ten if we don't count yours. There are already too many girls to begin with. The fewer you tap, the fewer will be disappointed."

I swallowed against my suddenly sandpapery throat. Here it was. The conversation I'd been dreading. I placed the card aside and folded my hands together.

"Yeah, about that only-eleven-members thing—"

"Don't even try it," Ivy said, pointing at me with the pen. "We said we were going to follow every point down to the letter."

I gritted my teeth and tilted my head. "I know, but—"

"There are no buts, Reed!" Ivy said, scrambling to her feet. "You promised we were going to honor the book, the original sisters. You can't go back on that now."

"But Ivy, there are only fifteen of us," I said, tilting my head back to look up at her. "What's the big deal if we let in four more? The whole reason I wanted to do this was to keep Billings together, not throw people out."

"I don't understand," Ivy said, pursing her lips as she crossed her arms over her slim chest. "If this is just about keeping Billings together, why am I even here?"

I shrugged and looked down at the heavy note cards spread before me. "Is it wrong to want to hang out with all of my friends together?" I said, looking up at her again. "Including you?"

Ivy rolled her eyes and let her hands droop at her sides. "God. Sometimes I forget how mushy you are."

"What?" I blurted, half offended, half laughing.

"You are!" She sat down again with a smile, shaking her head. "Listen to you. You sound like Anne of Green Gables or something."

"That was one of my favorite books as a kid," I conceded, toying with one of the pens. I used to fantasize about being whisked away from my family and adopted by stern-but-kind Marilla Cuthbert and sweet old Thomas. Anne's life might have been a bit of a struggle—especially before she went to the Island—but it was a freaking cakewalk compared to having a drug-addicted mother with violent mood swings and a penchant for guilt trips.

Thank God she was better now.

"I was more into Stephen King," Ivy replied.

I narrowed my eyes. "That explains a *lot*."

"Shut up, Anne Shirley." Ivy laughed and tossed the pen at me.

My phone beeped with a text.

Upton: Sorry for the delay. Math not my forte. Is approx 515 days. NOW will u tell me what ur wearing?

"What's with the blush?" Ivy asked, angling to see the phone. "Is it a *boy*?" she teased.

"Kind of," I said. "Well, yeah, he's a boy. I met him in St. Barths. When I wasn't, you know—"

"Left for dead on a deserted island?" she said, raising one eyebrow.

"Yeah. His name's Upton." I sighed, my heart feeling suddenly heavy as I looked down at the text.

Ivy twirled her pen between two fingers. "What's wrong?"

I leaned back on my hands, my phone in my lap. "It's just . . . it was fun while it lasted and everything, but he's in England and I'm here. . . . I think it was more of a transitional thing. But I really like him and we said that if neither one of us had a boyfriend or girlfriend by spring break, we'd go to Italy."

"Italy? Damn, girl," Ivy said, impressed. "The only place Josh has taken me is the house on the Cape."

Instantly, my throat crowded with jealousy. What was wrong with me? Here I was showing off about my amazing semiboyfriend and I still wanted *hers*. How selfish could I be? I picked up the phone again, hit the reply button and texted back.

Gray shorts and Easton T. Sorry it's not sexier. But it is hot in here, if that helps. :)

His reply came in seconds.

You = sexy in anything.

I smiled. Even thousands of miles away, Upton was good for the self-esteem.

"Got any pictures?" Ivy asked.

I scrolled to a photo of Upton I'd taken on the beach the day before we'd left the island. He looked insanely hot in plaid madras shorts with no shirt, the ring on his necklace glinting in the sunlight, his light brown hair tousled with ocean water. Ivy whistled.

"Okay. Next Christmas I'm going to St. Barths," she joked.

"Well, you can tell everyone I said hi, because I'm never going back there again." I powered my phone down and set it on my bed behind me.

Ivy looked up at me tentatively through her lashes, tapping her palm with the end of her pen. "Do you want to talk about it?" she asked. "What happened on that island, I mean. It must have been so freaking scary."

A huge rock settled in the center of my chest as the memories of the ordeal came back to me rapid-fire. "Not really," I said, neatening the pile of finished invites, my fingers suddenly trembling. "I'd rather just forget it ever happened, honestly. But thanks for asking."

"I understand," she said. "I didn't want to talk about the shooting for a while either." She leaned forward across her legs, reaching for one of the blank envelopes, then suddenly winced and fell back again. Her hand, still holding the pen, hovered over her stomach. Hot white guilt flooded my veins.

"Are you okay?" I asked. "Do you need something?"

"No. I'm good," she said, then laughed. "So much for not talking about it."

"Yeah," I said, because I couldn't think of anything else to say that

wouldn't be awkward. I handed her the envelope she'd been reaching for. My throat was so tight I could hardly breathe. "Okay," I said,
looking Ivy in the eye. "Eleven members it is."

"Yeah?" she asked, taking a deep, faltering breath.

I felt another surge of guilt and nodded.

"Yeah. There must have been some reason Elizabeth Williams
chose that number," I said, looking over at the book, which sat atop
my desk. "I may never know what it was, but it was important to her.
And it's important to you, too."

Ivy looked at me and smiled, blushing. "Okay, Anne Shirley."

"If you keep calling me that, *you're* not going to get tapped," I
told her.

Ivy raised her hands in surrender. "Fine. I'm done. Now let's write
these things up already. My butt's starting to go numb."

"Right. Let's do this," I said, resting another blank invitation atop
my chemistry book.

Carefully I started to write out Noelle's name.

Miss Noelle Lange
The honor of your presence is requested.
9:35 p.m. Friday night
Hull Hall
The basement
Enter by the south side window. Come alone.
Yours in sisterhood,
BLS

When I finished filling out the information, I held it up to check my work. A tingling of uncertainty wove through me and I wondered, just for a second, if we wouldn't be better off if she did turn us down. Already four people weren't going to get in. If Noelle bailed, it would be only three. The fewer casualties, the better, right?

Ivy handed me a freshly written envelope and I placed the invite inside, unsure of what to hope for. Noelle was the only one who could make the choice. I just hoped she made the right one, for all of us.

The weather was bright and crisp as Ivy and I walked across campus together to the post office to mail our taps. It was still early, the main green nearly empty. My heart was a ball of nervous excitement, and every time I looked at Ivy, she was grinning as stupidly as I was. We were really doing it. We were about to make our first real step in bringing back the Billings Literary Society. I had to press my lips together to keep from laughing out loud.

Ivy yanked open the door to the post office, letting me slip inside before her. I hurried over to the "Campus Mail Only" slot and stood next to it, impatiently waiting for her to catch up. My heart pounded like I was lining up to kick a penalty shot in the last minute of the biggest soccer game of my life.

"This is it," I said, as Ivy paused facing me. I pulled my stack of pristine ivory-colored envelopes out of my bag and held them in both hands.

Ivy looked me dead in the eye, clutching her half of the invites, grinning. Her hair was pulled back in a tight ponytail, highlighting her pale skin and red lips. "This is where it all begins."

We nodded, took a breath, and slipped the envelopes into the slot. Then we stood there for a moment, staring at it.

"Well. That was anticlimactic," I said.

"Coffee Carma?" she suggested.

"Sounds good."

We turned and nearly walked right into Noelle Lange. Both of us froze. I felt like my boyfriend had just caught me with another guy. Where the hell had she come from and how had she done it so stealthily?

"Hey, Reed," she said. Then she looked down her nose. "Ivy."

"Noelle," Ivy said, lowering her voice a few octaves in a mocking way.

I bit down on my tongue to keep from giggling. Noelle's eyes narrowed.

"You two have certainly been spending a lot of time together," Noelle said, striding past us to her mailbox. She was wearing tall brown boots, the tops of which disappeared beneath the hem of her belted, camel-colored wool coat. Girl owned more coats than I had pairs of shoes. "Lunch and dinner yesterday. Every period between classes . . ."

"Yeah, well, we're friends," I said. I had caught a couple of strange looks from the Billings Girls when Ivy and I had found our own table yesterday at the dining hall, but I figured they would all understand what was going on soon enough.

"Friends?" Noelle arched one brow as she worked the combination lock. "What on earth do you two have in common?" she asked. "Aside from an intimate knowledge of Josh Hollis, of course."

Ivy's jaw dropped open. I almost threw up on my shoes. She did *not* just go there.

"Oh, I don't know. We've both been backstabbed by you," Ivy shot back, her dark eyes aflame. "We've both been deserted by Billings on occasion."

Noelle smirked as she popped open the small gold door. "Interesting that those are your bonding points, considering what you've been doing behind closed doors."

Ivy and I exchanged a look. How did Noelle have any idea what we'd been doing? But then, she knew everything, didn't she? She'd been reminding me of that since the first day I met her. Noelle extracted her mail and blithely flipped through it before slamming the door of her box closed.

"Let me make one thing perfectly clear, Ivy," she said, walking casually toward us. She tucked the mail into her bag and lifted her brown hair over her shoulder. "You were not Billings material then, and you are not Billings material now."

She delivered this criticism calmly, matter-of-factly, like she was reporting on the weather. Ivy's ivory skin turned red so fast I actually flinched.

"You guys, listen, I know you've got some issues," I said, looking from one angry face to the other. "But can't you just try to get along? For me?"

It was as if I hadn't even spoken. As if I wasn't even there. The two of them simply stared at each other for a few seconds, before Ivy finally turned on her heel and headed for the door.

"I'll be outside, Reed," she said, shoving it open with one hand.

Noelle snorted a laugh. I turned to look at her.

"What is your problem?" I demanded.

"The problem is, Reed, she never should have been invited to join in the first place," Noelle replied. She shook her head and sighed, as if I was just so naïve. "I hope you didn't show her the book."

My heart switched places with my stomach. "Why do you care?"

"I don't. But I imagine that the person who left that thing for you wouldn't want you sharing it with outsiders," Noelle replied, adjusting the strap on her brown leather bag.

The door swung open and a pair of freshman girls walked in, chatting loudly. The moment they saw Noelle and I there, facing off, they stopped in their tracks, turned around, and walked right back out. Our reputation was just that intimidating, I guess, but I hardly cared. I was too busy fretting about what might happen if Noelle was right. What if whoever had given me the book was somehow keeping tabs on me and knew I'd included a non–Billings Girl in the proceedings? Would they take the book back?

I saw Noelle watching me out of the corner of her eye.

"Whatever," I said, not wanting her to see me sweat. "If you don't want to be involved, you shouldn't be commenting on how I do things."

Noelle smiled her knowing smile. "You're right. I have better things to do with my time."

Then she turned her back on me and started for the door. Searing hot frustration bubbled up from my very core.

"It's going to be amazing," I said. "At some point, you're going to be sorry you turned me down."

Noelle paused. She turned around and looked me in the eye. "Have fun playing pretend with your little friend." Then she whipped around again and walked out.

THE POTENTIALS

Candlelight flickered on the basement walls of Hell Hall, casting eerie shadows along the hulking piles of ancient wooden desks and rickety, broken chairs. This was, apparently, the place all Easton Academy furniture came to die, but tonight, it was going to play host to the start of something new. Something amazing. Something of which the teachers and administrators, who had their offices upstairs, would never approve.

I sat atop a huge metal desk, which Ivy and I had covered with one of the old, dusty, burgundy-colored curtains we'd found in the closet. We'd used the rest of them to cover up the piles of furniture to make the room look slightly cozier. Ivy was perched at one of the fourteen desks we'd arranged in a semicircle facing me.

Tiffany arrived first. She dropped down onto the gritty floor with the dexterity of the ace basketball player she was, frowned at the covered furniture, then took a seat. Rose was next. She peeked inside the window, smiled when she saw me, then turned around and backed through the window, dangling by her hands for a second before she let go. Lorna pretty much fell through sideways and crashed to the floor with an "oomph." Tiffany, Rose, and I jumped up to see if she was okay, while Ivy rolled her eyes and shook her head.

"I'm fine. I'm fine," Lorna whispered. Which, aside from the dirt smear on her camel coat and her obvious embarrassment, she was.

The girls arrived separately at perfect five-minute intervals. We'd planned it that way; it was Friday night, and we didn't want to generate suspicion in any security guards, teachers, or students who might be loitering in the vicinity. After Lorna came Vienna. Then Missy, Astrid, Kiki, London, Amberly, Shelby, and Portia. They all made it through the window unscathed, except for a scraped hand here or a torn hem there. Constance was one of the last to arrive. She fumbled through the window, plummeted to the floor, and fell right on her ass. Portia, who was closest to the window, snorted a laugh but went to help. Red-faced, Constance grabbed Portia's hand, scrambled to her feet, and looked around. When her eyes fell on me she visibly brightened and relaxed.

"Hey, Reed!" she said in full voice.

"Shhhhh!" the rest of the girls replied.

Constance's blush deepened. She quickly took the empty desk next to Astrid, which creaked loudly as she sat down and sort of listed to the side. Constance braced her feet on the floor and held on to the desk for dear life, clearly terrified of making even more of a scene.

Five minutes passed. I looked at the window. No shadows. No

footfalls. My eyes met Ivy's. Tiffany shifted impatiently in her seat. Shelby cleared her throat and checked her iPhone. Vienna, London, and Portia started to whisper and giggle. The solemn atmosphere we had attempted to create with the late-night meeting time and candles was deteriorating fast. The girls were starting to grow restless. And from the direction of their glances, I could also tell that the Billings Girls were wondering why Ivy was there. I glanced at the window again, growing antsy, and held my watch closer to the candle on my desk.

Nine forty-five. Noelle's designated time had been nine thirty-five. It seemed Miss Lange had, in fact, moved on.

"All right, it looks like we're all here," I began, pushing myself off the desk to stand before them. Everyone looked startled, I'm sure pondering the distinct lack of Noelle. "For the past week, many of us have been wondering what's to become of Billings. Yes, the building is gone, but for those of us who lived there, being in Billings wasn't just about the house. It was about us. Our friendship, our sisterhood, our support of one another."

I paused. Every pair of eyes in the room was riveted on me.

"Well, I think I've found a way to preserve the spirit of Billings." I turned to slide the book off the desk, practically giddy in anticipation of their reactions to what I was about to say.

That was when the window hinges squeaked. Everyone turned to look. Noelle's black Gucci boots backed through the opening. She eased herself down, her hands clutching the sill, and dropped to the floor, her knees barely bending as her shoes hit the ground. She dusted off the front of her black coat, lifted her hair over her shoulder, and smiled.

"What did I miss?"

She'd shown. She'd actually shown. I looked at Ivy. Her lips were pursed and her entire body looked tense. She was going to get up and walk out. I could feel it in my bones. If I had to choose between her and Noelle . . .

Well, I didn't want to have to do that.

"I thought you weren't coming," I said to Noelle.

"Are you kidding? Who could ignore an invite like this?" she said, tossing her cream envelope down on my desk like it was a random scrap of paper. She eyed the book clutched in my arms, my teacher's desk, the students' desks and chairs gathered in front of me, and gave a wry smile. Then she turned and sat down in the very last desk at the end of the arc.

"Well, Teach?" she said, arching an eyebrow. "How about you educate us on this secret society of yours?"

"Secret society?" Astrid gasped.

"What? That's so cool!" Kiki added.

Suddenly everyone was whispering, their chairs creaking and shifting. I glared at Noelle. She'd just swooped in here and snatched my big announcement right out from under me.

"Oops," she mouthed.

I rolled my eyes. "You guys! *Quiet down!*" I whisper-shouted.

Everyone shushed everyone else and soon they were all facing me.

"Okay," I said, taking a deep breath. "Yes, we are all here to talk about forming a secret society. The Billings Literary Society, to be exact. It was started back in 1915 and was functioning all the way up until Easton absorbed Billings School for Girls in the 1970s."

"How do you know all this?" Missy interrupted, her nostrils flaring in annoyance.

"Someone left this for me," I said, lifting the book. "It's the history of the society."

Tiffany, Rose, and Astrid all sat forward, eying the book with a covetous gleam in their eyes.

"We may not be able to rebuild our house, but we *can* keep the spirit of Billings alive at Easton," I said.

Just then, a door opened and closed upstairs. My heart vaulted into my throat and everyone froze. Amberly reached out and grabbed Kiki's arm. Footsteps slowly crossed the hall overhead. I closed my eyes and prayed that whoever it was hadn't seen the candlelight, hadn't heard our voices. There were a few more footsteps. A slam. Then nothing. I looked down the row of terrified eyes, stopping at Noelle. She was glaring at me so hard I could practically read her thoughts: If this stupid little project of mine got her expelled, she was going to eviscerate me.

Ouch.

"Um, Reed?" Kiki said. "I vote that if we're going to keep meeting like this, we don't do it here."

Everyone relaxed a bit, laughing quietly.

"Don't worry. If everything goes as planned, we'll only have to meet here one more time," I told them.

"So?" Noelle said, crossing her arms over her chest as she sat back. "What *is* the plan?"

"Well, before we talk about anything else, I should tell you that the BLS will only have eleven members," I said, my heart beating nervously. "That's a really big rule in the book, and I've decided to adhere to the book completely."

"But there are fifteen people here. For *some* reason," Portia said, eyeing Ivy snidely.

"I know," I replied, ignoring her pointed tone. I swallowed hard. "Four of us will not get in."

This announcement was met with dead silence. I glanced nervously at Ivy. She lifted her chin and gave me a confident look.

"How are you going to decide who doesn't get in?" Tiffany asked.

I let out a breath I didn't realize I was holding. "The book outlines three tasks that each prospective member has to complete. The pledge mistress—that would be me—grades them. The four lowest scorers would be cut. That's how they did it back in the day, and that's how we're going to do it now."

They all exchanged dubious looks. I half expected Shelby or Portia to walk out at this point. They weren't exactly the type of people who looked forward to being tested in any way. And I'd always had the impression that Billings didn't mean as much to them as it did to the rest of us.

"So, if you're all in . . ." I paused to give them one last chance to bail. But no one moved. "The first task will be held here on Monday at midnight. This is the knowledge task. I can't give you the particulars of how you'll be tested, but you're going to want to scrounge up your Easton handbooks and study them. Carefully."

Shelby scrunched up her face like I was insane. "I don't even know where that thing is." Which made sense. She was, after all, a senior, and the handbook was something we were given out the first day we arrived on campus. Most people forgot about it about ten seconds later.

"I'm sure you can get a new one in the office. Or better yet, take one out of the library. Asking Double H's secretary for one might arouse suspicion."

"Speaking of Double H . . . wasn't there a little announcement about the banning of social clubs?" Vienna said, raising her hand as she spoke.

"Yeah. What does that mean for us?" London added.

There was another creak overhead. We all held our breath. Then a set of keys jangled and the front door slammed so hard some of the furniture piles shook. I looked my friends in the eye, one by one, and summoned the firmest tone I could muster in the midst of my trepidation.

"It means," I said, "that we're going to have to be very, *very* careful."

THE RULES

"Okay, so why are we here again?" Graham asked, coming up behind me and Ivy as we walked into the gym for the girls' basketball game. "I mean, it's Saturday night. Sat-ur-day night!" he added, doing a twist move with his hips. "Shouldn't we be, like, I don't know . . . party-ing?"

Ivy and I laughed. I was about to answer when Gage and Trey Prescott, Josh's roommate, joined us. Gage slapped one hand down on Graham's shoulder and leaned in close.

"Dude. Look around," he said. "What's more of a party than ten half-naked girls, sweating and chasing balls?"

"Gross!" Ivy protested.

"Please don't let him corrupt you," I said to Graham. "You're such a nice guy."

Graham stood up straight and tilted his head. "Still. The man *does* have a point."

The three guys laughed as they jostled through the door ahead of us. I rolled my eyes at Ivy and took one of the blue-and-gold pom-poms the freshmen were handing out just inside the door. Easton was playing the Barton School, and Tiffany, Shelby, and Missy were all on the team. Normally this was the kind of thing Ivy would have steered clear of, not being a big school spirit girl and all that, but I had convinced her it would be a good thing to support our prospective sisters.

"So. I've been thinking about the first task," I said under my breath, running the silky plastic of the mini pom-pom through my fingers. "And I think it might be better if we—"

"I don't want to hear about it," Ivy said, pausing at the end of the jam-packed bleachers. At my old school, Croton High, a girls' basketball game wouldn't have drawn much of a crowd, but here at Easton, where we were all campus-bound in the dead of winter, it was like a rave. Gage and Trey had joined Josh and the other guys at the top of the center bleachers. As I found them, Josh met my eyes, then quickly looked away. Graham, I noticed, had broken off from them and was sitting with Sawyer a couple of sections away.

"What do you mean you don't want to hear about it?" I waved at Constance, who was sitting a few rows in front of Josh, wearing an Easton sweatshirt over a plaid skirt. She was surrounded by Kiki, Astrid, Missy, Amberly, and Rose. She smiled and waved back, but her always sweet and welcoming face turned a tad sour when she saw that Ivy was with me.

"I want to be tested just like everyone else," Ivy told me, holding her ground as a couple of Barton guys tried to nudge us forward onto the bleachers. "I already know more than I should. But if we're going to do this thing right, you should test me and make sure I make the cut."

The Barton guys finally got the hint that we weren't budging any time soon and went around us. One of them blatantly checked out Ivy as he went by and she smiled back at him.

Geez. You have a boyfriend, remember? I glanced at Josh again. This time his gaze was trained on the court, where the girls were finishing up their pregame warm-up and jogging for the benches. I took a breath and told myself to focus.

"That's insane." I looked into Ivy's eyes and realized she wasn't kidding. "Ivy, I need your help. How am I going to set up these tests and administer them and judge the results all on my own? That's impossible."

"Yeah, but it's the rules," Ivy said under her breath. "You're the Elizabeth Williams here, Reed. Once you have a membership, you'll have all the help you need, but for this one, you're going to have to make the decisions."

"If you're getting tested, then I should be too." I said, starting up the steps.

She grabbed my arm and pulled me back down, tugging me into the corner by the fire extinguisher. Over the loudspeakers, the national anthem started to play.

"Whoever left you that book chose you," she said. "You're the one person who gets a pass."

"Okay, fine," I said. "You can do the tasks. But if you fail any of them, I will personally kick your butt."

She smirked. "I would expect nothing less."

The players gathered at the center of the court for the tip-off. Cheers of "Go Easton!" and "Let's go Barton!" erupted from the stands as sneakers squeaked on the freshly waxed floors.

"I'm going to go get a soda," Ivy told me. "Save me a seat."

"Okay." I sighed, suddenly heavy with the full weight of the Billings Literary Society on my shoulders. "I'll be up there with Constance and those guys."

"Got it," Ivy said with a nod.

She paused to let a crowd of Barton fans through, their faces painted red and white. As the buzzer commenced the game, I started up the bleachers, carefully avoiding fingers and toes and book bags. Halfway up, I felt someone watching me and glanced toward the top bleacher. Josh. He quickly looked away, and a lump formed in my throat. I wished I could just go up there and join him. Hang out with him, talk to him, just be near him. But I couldn't. Feeling suddenly conspicuous, I slid into the aisle where my friends were sitting. Constance made room for me on the bench next to her, slipping her backpack onto the floor and her coat under her butt. I sat down and smiled, concentrating on not looking back at Josh again.

"Thanks."

"No problem," she said, tugging her thick, red ponytail over her opposite shoulder. "Where'd Ivy go?"

"To get something to drink," I replied, keeping one eye on the game.

"Oh. That's good."

Constance continued to fiddle with her hair. Then she uncrossed and recrossed her legs half a dozen times and sighed.

"What's wrong?" I asked finally.

"Nothing! It's just . . ." She turned toward me, her back toward the other girls, and lowered her voice. "You planned this whole thing with her, didn't you? The BLS?" she said, her whisper dropping to barely audible. "Her and Noelle."

My heart skipped a tentative beat.

"Noelle had nothing to do with it."

A Barton player with a frizzy blond ponytail scored a sweet three; half the crowd went nuts.

"But they both knew about it before the rest of us," Constance whispered as the cheers died down. "We could all tell."

"I needed someone to help me figure it all out," I admitted, keeping my eye on the game. Tiffany stole the ball and raced down the court, executing a perfect layup. I clapped my hands as the Easton side cheered. "Noelle said no so I asked Ivy."

Constance swallowed, her lips pulled back almost as if she were trying not to throw up. "Ivy Slade."

My gut tightened. Suddenly I knew exactly where this was going.

"Constance, I—"

"She's not even a Billings Girl," Constance said, ducking her head. "I mean, why would you ask her instead of, like . . . Kiki or Astrid or—"

"You?" I finished.

"No! No . . . I mean . . . well, yeah," Constance said with a shrug. "Why not me? I mean, I thought we were friends."

"We are," I said. "It's just, Ivy . . ."

How was I supposed to explain this? Was I really going to say that Ivy was stronger? Smarter? Better at keeping a secret?

"Ivy was . . . She was really depressed after the shooting," I lied. "I just felt like she needed something, you know? Like a project? Something to make her feel like she was useful and part of something."

Constance's eyes widened. "Really?"

She was so gullible I felt even guiltier for lying. "Yeah. But don't say anything about it, okay? She's still pretty sensitive."

"Okay. I get it," Constance said eagerly. If there was one thing she loved, it was to feel included, to be brought into someone's confidence.

"Constance, you know not to tell anyone about this, right?" I said, placing my hand on hers. "Not even Whit?"

Constance rolled her eyes. "Please. I know what the word *secret* means, Reed."

I sure hoped so.

She shifted in her seat and looked out at the court. "That's so nice of you to do that for Ivy. Especially since she's with Josh and everything. You're, like, a saint!"

I gave her a stiff smile.

Just then, Ivy joined us, dropping down on the bench next to me and taking a swig of her Coke. "All right, explain this game to me," she said. "I know you're supposed to get the ball through the hoop, but other than that I got nothing."

"I can explain it to you!" Constance offered, getting up and shooing me aside so she could sit next to Ivy.

I slid closer to Kiki and tried not to hang my head in shame. Now Constance was being nice to Ivy because she thought the girl was depressed? Good one, Reed.

But so what? I'd only lied to spare Constance's feelings. The one little lie wouldn't matter.

During a lull in the noise, I heard my phone beep and fished it out of my bag. It was a text from Upton.

Haven't heard from you in a while. Are we still friends? :)

My heart clenched and I looked around at the Easton crowd. Ivy and Constance were chatting with their heads bent close together. The rest of the girls were cheering as Tiffany set up the next play at center court, dribbling the ball in front of her. And behind me, I could practically feel Josh's presence. Feel his eyes on the back of my neck.

Just my imagination. It was just me wishing I was as important to him now as I'd once been.

From the corner of my eye, I glanced at Ivy. She was completely focused on the game. Slowly, I turned around, trying to make it seem like I was just looking for someone in the crowd.

And Josh was staring right at me. My heart stopped. He held my gaze for a long moment. A *very* long moment. I couldn't breathe. Couldn't think. All I wanted to do was grab him and pull him out of here and kiss him. Then finally, slowly, he looked past me at the court. The moment passed, but my pulse continued to race.

My throat completely dry, I turned around again and looked down at my phone. It was possible that Josh and I would never be together again. But I was starting to think that my getting over him was completely *im*possible. My heart heavy, my fingers trembling, I texted Upton back.

Of course we're still friends. but would u hate me 4ever if i said "just friends?"

I held my breath, fretting over his reply. It came almost instantly.

Could never hate u. And can never have enuf hot American friends.

I laughed, relieved, and texted back a thank-you, then tucked my phone away and tried to concentrate on the game. At least one relationship on my life was now clearly defined. Now if only I could figure out the rest of them, I'd be golden.

LIGHT READING

"Did you guys know that Mitchell and Micah Easton had a sister? Her name was Marianne and she married this French guy against her father's wishes and moved to Paris," Constance gushed, leaning over the table at the solarium on Sunday night.

"I like the girl already," Astrid put in.

She was kicked back, her big black boots on the marble table, a huge hardcover copy of *Jane Eyre* open in front of her. Tucked inside of it was her Easton Handbook, open to a back page having to do with Easton's prized historical objects. The old bell, the paintings in the art cemetery, the cornerstone from Gwendolyn Hall, the oldest building at Easton . . . at least until last semester's fire leveled it. The cornerstone was now encased in glass in the library.

"Do you think anyone is wondering what we're doing?" London whispered, leaning over the table as she looked around.

Constance, Kiki, Lorna, Missy, London, Vienna, and Rose also had their handbooks hidden inside novels from the list inscribed at the back of the Billings Literary Society book. The list had been added to throughout the years, starting with Thomas Paine's *Common Sense* and ending with *Fear of Flying* by Erica Jong. It was our way of paying homage to the original Billings Girls, and it gave the handbooks the perfect camouflage. Any teacher might have thought it was odd if a table full of coffee-sipping girls were poring over the Easton handbook—especially considering we were all juniors and seniors. Library books, however, were more of a common sight around here.

"They're probably wondering what *you're* doing since you haven't taken out a library book since your Clifford the Big Red Dog days," Vienna joked.

London shoved Vienna's arm and clucked her tongue but laughed as she sat back again.

Surreptitiously I glanced around the octagonal solarium. Sandwiched between the Coffee Carma counter on the far wall and the bay of windows that overlooked the now darkened campus were about twenty other students. Some were curled into the high-backed chairs and a few sat chatting on couches and laughing over texts. A group of senior girls at the next table over were eyeing us with what could only be called disdain. I wondered just how many people here thought that the razing of Billings was justified.

Then my gaze fell on Diana and her friend Shane Freundel. I lifted my hand in a wave, which they reciprocated with a smile. They had always been so intrigued by Billings. Were they annoyed that it had been torn down—that they wouldn't get that last chance to live

there as seniors? Maybe next year, after the current seniors graduated, I would invite them and Sonal to be in the new class of potentials.

Just as I was about to turn back to my book, I spotted Josh coming
through the doorway with Trey. The moment he saw me, he turned
red, ducked his head, and veered off toward the coffee counter. Clearly
confused, Trey hesitated for a moment, then followed.

My face burned. Was the idea of saying hello to me so very awful?

"I can't believe they actually wanted to tear down the original
library in the eighties," Rose said, reaching for her coffee. "I love that
building."

"I know. Good thing the Whittakers put a stop to it," Kiki said.
"Thank your boyfriend for us, C."

Constance beamed and grabbed her phone. "I'll text him right
now."

I forced a smile, trying to put Josh out of my mind, and scanned
the page of the handbook in front of me, searching out tough but fair
questions. As I jotted down a note about the number of books housed
within the Easton library, I felt a shift in the solarium's jovial vibe.

"Incoming," Kiki whispered.

Headmaster Hathaway was strolling toward our table, all hip-
casual in a cashmere sweater-over-shirt combo and flat-front pants.
He had a quizzical look on his face. My friends pulled their books a
bit closer, drawing the thick tomes into their laps or holding them
directly in front of their faces.

"Good evening, ladies," he greeted us, standing just over Rose's shoulder. Rose slipped her handbook from her copy of *The Bostonians* and placed it in her lap under the table. "Getting in a little light reading?"

Every pair of eyes slid toward me. I closed my copy of *Clarissa* and placed it flat on the table, folding my hands over it.

"Actually, we're thinking about forming a literary club," I said.

A few of my friends tensed. But the closer my words were to the truth, the harder it would be to peg them as outright lies.

Over the past year and a half I'd learned a few things from Noelle and Cheyenne. Even Ariana and Sabine. God help me.

The headmaster rubbed his chin.

"Interesting. Are your teachers not giving you enough class work? Because I can have a chat with them about that if you like," he said, a twinkle in his eye.

"Oh no. Our workload is fine," Kiki said, dropping her heavy copy of *War and Peace* on the table with a thud. "It's just that we Billings Girls *love* to read. It's kind of what we're known for."

Everyone, including me, barely held in the laughter.

"Did they not tell you that about us?" Astrid put in. "We are extraordinarily dedicated to the advancement of our intellect."

The headmaster furrowed his brow. He was no longer in on the joke, and he clearly didn't like the feeling.

"Well. That's refreshing to hear," he said after a beat. Then he cleared his throat and straightened his shoulders. "But let me remind you all that the Billings Girls no longer exist. You are all simply students of Easton Academy now."

"Oh yes," Missy said, pressing her lips together to keep from smiling. "We're aware."

"Very aware," Lorna added, smoothing her freshly straightened hair over her shoulder.

"Good," he said. Then he gave me a quick nod and a smile. "Enjoy your reading."

We all held our breath as he walked away. Somehow we managed to wait until he left the solarium, fresh cappuccino in hand, before we doubled over laughing.

THE FIRST TASK

At midnight on Monday, everyone gathered once again in the basement of Hell Hall. I'd gotten there early to rehang the dark drapes
over the furniture, but this time there would be no light aside from
that generated by the large white candle I held in my hands. The room
was so hushed I could hear the wick burning slowly down. Standing
in a wide circle around me were the fourteen potentials, all of them
dressed in head-to-toe white, as instructed. Which, given the fact
that it was January, couldn't have been easy. There were a few mini-
dresses, a couple pairs of wrinkled linen pants. Constance was wearing a floor-length white flannel nightgown that made her look about
eight years old. Kiki sported a tank top and white boxers. Tiffany kept
her white coat buttoned over whatever she was wearing underneath.
Noelle, of course, had donned a white silk dress that looked as if it
had just been whisked off some runway model mid—fashion show and
flown in for the occasion.

I took a breath and looked down at my candle. The book had
instructed that I pose a question to a prospective, then tilt the candle
over that person's hand as they answered. If an answer took more
than five seconds, I was to drip hot wax on that person's hand.

The very idea had kept me up at night. It seemed 1915 had been
a mite closer to medieval torture times. So I'd decided to change it
slightly—update it to fit with the times. Upon their arrival, each of the
potentials had been given a book of matches. Lorna turned hers over
and over in her fingers.

I glanced at my watch. It was one minute past twelve.

"You have all gathered here in confidence to have your worthiness
tested," I began.

A couple of people flinched at the sound of my voice. My candle
flickered. I took a breath and told myself to chill.

"I have arranged you in order of your seniority at Easton," I said,
turning to face Noelle. "The eldest will be tested first."

Noelle smirked. My hand shook.

"You will light one match. I will pose my question. You must answer
correctly before the flame is extinguished," I instructed. This way, I
had figured, the time restriction would still be in place, and maybe a
few fingertips would be singed, but at least I wouldn't have to personally injure anyone. "A late answer will be marked as a wrong answer.
Each of you will be asked five questions in turn." I fixed each girl with
a brief stare. Amberly looked like she was about to pass out. "There
will be silence throughout this process. Only myself and the person
before the flame may speak."

It felt weird, speaking to my friends so formally, and they obviously felt it too. A few of them had to press their lips together to keep from laughing or smiling. This niggled at my nerves and I felt a sudden desire to just get this over with. Who was I to be doling out rules and regulations? To be running a meeting like this? I looked at Noelle again and my thoughts were reflected in her eyes.

My very bones burned with ire.

"Light your first match, plebe," I said, looking her directly in the eye. Which, I'll admit, took some serious effort.

"Reed, don't you think this is a tad . . . ill-advised?" Noelle replied. "We already torched Gwendolyn this year and I—"

"You will not speak until you are asked a question," I blurted forcefully.

Someone behind me took in a sharp breath. Noelle's jaw stiffened.

"Fine."

"Shh!" Vienna's eyes were wide as she shushed Noelle. I stood a bit taller, inflated with pride. At least I was intimidating *someone*. Noelle rolled her eyes but lit the match. Over the tiny flame, she eyed me with annoyed impatience.

"What is the acreage of the plot on which Easton Academy is sit—"

"Twenty square acres," she replied before I could even finish.

She blew out her match, dropped it on the floor, and lit another. I hesitated, thrown by the fact that a) I hadn't even finished the question b) she'd answered correctly and c) she'd already moved on.

"Um . . . in what year was the Billings School for Girls absorbed by Easton Acad—"

"Nineteen seventy-five," Noelle replied.

Flame extinguished. Flame ignited. This time, I was ready.

"The Easton chapel was constructed in the style of what religious sect?"

"Christian-Dutch reform," Noelle answered.

Crap. That was my hardest question. I felt myself start to give in. I should just give Noelle her gold star and move on. But I'd said five questions, and five it would be.

"How many men were in Easton's original graduating class?" I asked.

"Ten," she replied.

"What is the oldest building on the Easton Academy campus?" I asked.

"Well, it *was* Gwendolyn Hall until recently. Now it's the chapel," she replied.

She waved her fingers to extinguish the last match, then crossed her arms over her chest like she just couldn't wait to get out of there. I felt all trembly inside, as if I'd just confronted my worst enemy and failed. I turned to Tiffany, resolving to be tougher this time.

Faster, stronger, better. I couldn't remember where that motto came from, but now it was mine.

"How many former headmasters' portraits are currently hanging in the art cemetery?" I asked, my voice steady.

"Fifteen," Tiffany answered.

Slowly, I moved through the circle of potentials. Tiffany went five for five, as did Ivy. Vienna got four right. Portia nailed all five and Shelby got four, but London got only two correct and was tearful by the end of it. Suddenly I started to wonder what we were all doing here. Couldn't I just say, "Hey, let's form this secret society," and invite them all to join me?

I glanced shakily at Ivy. She narrowed her eyes slightly, urging me on. We were doing this to honor our sisters' memories. The ritual of it was important. The tradition mattered. These were the things that made the Billings Literary Society special. Succeeding at these tests would set our members apart.

Rose went five for five. Astrid too. Kiki answered hers even faster than Noelle had. Missy got four out of five. Lorna managed all five without breaking a sweat. Finally, I came to Constance, the last in the circle aside from Amberly. Constance grinned as she struck her first match.

It didn't light. She tried again. Again, nothing.

Noelle *tsk*ed impatiently. I shot her a silencing glare and she raised her hands in mock surrender. My shoulder muscles coiled at her total lack of reverence. If this was such a joke to her, why didn't she just leave?

I turned around again and focused on Constance. Finally, on the fifth try, the match lit, but Constance's hand was quaking and the grin was gone.

"The building that now houses the Easton gymnasium was originally constructed as what?" I asked.

Constance's eyes widened. My heart skipped a beat.

A civil war hospital, I told her telepathically. *A civil war hospital!*

The flame went out. "Ow." Constance shook her hand, then sucked on her fingertips. I felt sick to my stomach. No answer meant a wrong answer.

"Second question," I said, my voice quavering.

It took her three tries to get the match lit this time. Finally, the flame flickered to life, playing over her pale face. Her eyes were glassy with unshed tears and my heart constricted. My next question was even harder than the first. I couldn't do that to her. She needed to get her confidence back. Even as my conscience prattled on in my ear, telling me that fair was fair and that all the questions tonight had been hard, I knew what I had to do.

"In what year was Easton Academy founded?" I asked.

Someone scoffed. It was arguably the easiest question of the night.

"Nineteen fifty-eight," she answered.

I felt like a lollipop stick had lodged itself sideways in my throat.

"I mean, 1858," she corrected, then laughed nervously.

"Right." But according to the book, I had to mark it as wrong. The first answer was the final answer.

It took Constance six tries to get the next match lit.

"What were the first names of the founding brothers?" I asked.

Amberly's jaw dropped. I knew what she was thinking. Her questions had better be this easy.

But she didn't understand. Constance was the weakest of the bunch. Not when it came to friendship and loyalty and compassion, maybe, but when it came to self-confidence, to overcoming nerves, to being singled out in a crowd.

"Micah and Mitchell," Constance said confidently.

Right. Thank God. Only one try on the match this time.

"And their sister was named?"

"Ma—" Constance stopped. Her face turned green. She blinked up at the ceiling, her lips screwed up in concentration. "Mary—no. Maryyyyy . . . something."

Dammit. She knew this. I knew she knew it. She was the one who had told us all about her at the solarium that night. She had to remember this.

"Mary . . . Mary-Alice?" she said.

I swallowed hard. "Incorrect."

Her face crumpled. She blew out the match. And then she started to cry. My heart shattered into a thousand tiny pieces and fluttered to the floor. Lorna leaned over and put her arm around Constance, whispering something in her ear.

"Fifth question," I said, hating myself.

Lorna lit the match for Constance. Even though it was technically against the rules, I said nothing. Ivy blinked but remained silent.

"Name one of the original members of the Billings Literary Society."

They had all been given a list. My original intent had been to have her name all of them, but I wasn't about to go there.

"Theresa . . . Theresa Billings," Constance mumbled.

That, at least, was right.

It seemed to me that even the windows and desks and doors sighed with relief as Constance extinguished her final match. As I turned to Amberly, Constance continued to sniffle. I had to wonder if, through the years, the previous members of the BLS had endured nights like this one.

Suddenly I wasn't sure I had the nerve to administer the next two tasks—to put my friends through the wringer like this. I wasn't sure it was in me. Maybe whoever had left the book in my room had made a mistake. Noelle was much better suited to this type of leadership role. She was the one who could order people around without batting an eye. The one who always remained cool in the face of other people's raw emotions. This role was practically written for her.

So, as I caught sight of Constance's red eyes, I had to wonder why was I the one playing the part.

PINING

On Tuesday morning, I paused outside the food line in the dining hall, holding my tray of cereal and toast in front of me. The Billings tables were quiet. No animated conversation, no going over homework and paging through magazines. Everyone was staring at their food, not even acknowledging one another. I hesitated—told myself that we were all tired after sneaking back to our dorms at almost 2 a.m. That they weren't angry or disgruntled about the emotional roller coaster of the night before. But it was difficult to believe.

"Hey, Reed."

Sawyer startled me so badly my tray almost tipped.

"Sorry," he said, grimacing as I saved my bowl from going over the edge. Compared to how I felt, he looked insanely awake and happy, his eyes bright and his smile even brighter. He wore a green sweater under his coat and his dark blond hair fell forward over his forehead.

"S'okay," I said.

"Wanna sit together?" he asked, tilting his head toward an empty table.

I brightened instantly. An excuse for avoiding the obviously depressing vibe at my table, which *might* just be focused on me? "Sure," I said.

As I slid into a seat across from Sawyer I kept my eyes on the Billings Girls. Constance wasn't there. Nor were London, Vienna, or Amberly, who had gotten four out of five of her questions right. It was possible that London and Constance's absences had nothing to do with their embarrassment over being the two low scorers on the first task, but not likely. Vienna had probably run to Coffee Carma to get London her favorite vanilla spice latte and apple Danish to bring over to her room, and Constance was most likely huddled under the covers in Pemberly, replaying the whole awful episode over and over again in her mind.

I wished she were there so I could tell her she had plenty of chances to make it up. If she could ace the next two tasks, the first would barely count. And after last night, I had decided that the next two tasks were going to be easier than the first. More fun. More group-oriented. No more being put on the spot.

"Hey," Sawyer said. "Everything okay?"

My eyes darted back to him as he took a sip of coffee. He made a face and ripped open a sugar packet.

"Yeah. Sorry," I said, dipping my spoon into my Lucky Charms. "I just didn't sleep well last night."

"Re-*eed*! I have a surprise for you!" Ivy sang, walking over to our table in a whirl of red coat. She dropped her tray next to Sawyer's, whipped off her hat, and sat down. "I just got us passes to go off campus after classes today! We are going shopping." She picked up her bagel and glanced at Sawyer. "Hey, headmaster's son. How are ya?"

I blinked a few times. Her energy was so incongruent to my exhaustion and deep thoughts, I felt like I'd just been knocked off my chair.

"Um, fine," Sawyer said with a laugh. "You sure are a morning person."

"You know, usually I'm not," Ivy said thoughtfully. "But today I'm in a good mood."

At least *someone* was happy. Her lips were perfectly glossed, her lashes long and curled, her skin rosy. I felt ten times more tired just looking at her.

"Shopping?" I said. "For what?"

"I need to get a new dress for the dance," Ivy informed me.

"The dance. Right." I glanced at Sawyer, and he blushed and looked away.

Rose, who was passing by the table slowly, looking as out of it as I felt, paused. "What are you doing over here?"

"Sawyer asked me to sit with him," I said. "Want to join us?"

Rose looked over her shoulder at the Billings tables. "Okay."

She slid behind me and sat down, smoothing the skirt of her purple dress over her legs. "I'm Rose," she said to Sawyer. "You're one of the headmaster's sons."

Sawyer laughed under his breath. "Sawyer," he said, then looked at me. "What do I need to do to become something other than 'the headmaster's son'?" he joked.

"Streak in the class building during first period," Ivy suggested, her mouth half full. "That'll do it." She reached for her juice as Sawyer laughed. "So, Reed? Shopping tonight?"

"Sure," I said.

"Yay!" Ivy clapped her hands and took another bite of bagel.

"Why are you so awake?" Rose semiwhined, reaching for her coffee.

"Oh, you mean . . . oh." Ivy stopped, clearly realizing she shouldn't say anything out loud and took a sip of OJ. "I'm used to not sleeping. Ever since the . . . *accident* . . . it's just not something I do much of."

"Oh." I told myself I shouldn't feel guilty about this. It was not my fault. It was Sabine's. And to a lesser extent Josh's. But the fact that Ariana's crazy half-sister had targeted me because Ariana had ended up in an insane asylum after trying to kill me just couldn't be my fault. All I'd done was show up at Easton. The rest was on the insane blood pumping through the Osgood/DuLac veins.

"You can come, too, Rose," Ivy said brightly. "I could use a second and third opinion. Josh and I haven't really done the dress-up-and-go-out thing. At least not since I've been in the hospital. I want it to be perfect."

At the mention of Josh's name, my eyes went right to him. He was seated at a table with a bunch of his soccer buddies, leaned over someone's iPhone, looking at heaven knew what. There was a small red paint stain on the sleeve of his navy blue rugby shirt. For some reason, that tiny splotch made my heart hurt.

"Okay. I'm in," Rose said. She gave a huge yawn and stretched her arms over her head. "If I'm still awake then."

I smiled.

Back in their sophomore year, Ivy and Rose had been friends. Maybe the BLS would bring them back together.

The BLS. Wasn't that supposed to be my focus right now? Not Josh. Not romance. Not the things I couldn't have. I was supposed to be looking toward the future, not pining for the past. Maybe helping Ivy tonight would be just the thing to help me let him go and move on.

I had some shopping to do for the second task anyway. Maybe today in class I could brainstorm some solid ideas on how to turn the depressing vibe at the Billings tables around with Loyalty Night. This whole secret-society thing was supposed to be fun, but so far, it seemed like Ivy was the only one having any.

THE SECOND TASK

We met for the second task in the common room on the ground floor of Pemberly Hall. As my friends walked in, I could tell they were surprised and a bit nervous at the public arena, the brightness of the room, the fact that it wasn't the dead of night. It was dark out, of course. In mid-January it got dark at five o'clock. But we'd just come from dinner. People were still up and about on campus. Several of them were even hanging out in the common room, watching us with interest as we settled in on the uneven pentagon of couches I'd arranged in the center of the room.

"What's this? A fifth-grade slumber party?" Noelle asked, dropping her coat and bag over the back of the longest couch and settling herself in. On the table in front of her were open bags of M&M's, Reese's peanut butter cups, pretzels and Tostitos, a jar of pineapple salsa, plus several cans of Coke and bottles of water from the vending machine.

"My budget doesn't exactly support Godiva and Perrier," I said, standing in the wedge between the arms of two love seats until all fourteen girls had arrived.

"So, what're we going to do tonight?" Missy asked, looking down her nose at the spread. "Cut open our palms and make blood vows over an empty calorie fest or something?"

"No," I said, taking the last seat, which happened to be right next to her. "Tonight, we are going to have a little fun."

I picked up the brown bag from the floor and dumped out seventy-five safety pins on the table. Each was tied with a tiny dark brown or baby blue ribbon—the official colors of the BLS. I'd spent half the night last night making them, and my fingertips still smarted from the effort.

"Everyone take five pins and attach them to your person," I said.

They looked at one another dubiously, but Constance dove right in and started pinning the ribbons to her chest. I did the same, trying to show them that I was, in fact, serious. Once everyone had grudgingly done as they were told—Noelle the grudgingliest of all—I grabbed a bottle of water and a handful of M&M's for strength. I had a feeling the girls were going to think "cheese" was my middle name after I explained this task.

"We're going to play a little friendship game," I told them.

"Oh my God! It *is* a fifth-grade sleepover!" London trilled.

Vienna clapped her hands, all hyper, and everyone laughed. I smiled gratefully. At least they hadn't gotten up and walked out.

"Everyone's going to have some munchies and soda and we're all just going to hang out and talk," I said, crunching away on my chocolate.

"About what?" Kiki asked, drawing her heavy boots up under her on the couch.

"About us," I said, lifting a shoulder. "Good memories, bad memories, funny stories . . ." I trailed off as my eyes fell on Ivy, who was looking suddenly uncomfortable. Right. She wasn't technically one of us. But she'd known Portia, Rose, Tiffany, Noelle, Vienna, Shelby, and London for a long time. Surely they had some mutual stories that didn't involve putting her grandmother in the hospital. "If, during the conversation, you overhear a sister—I mean *friend*," I amended, glancing up as Jillian walked by on her way to the stairs, "say something bad about another friend, you can take one of that person's pins for yourself. The idea, obviously, is to say only good things about each other, but also to keep an ear open for disparaging comments. The game ends when one person has lost all their pins. Which hopefully won't happen at all."

"Wow. Who came up with this lameness?" Missy groused, shifting in her seat.

"I think it sounds like fun!" Rose put in with a bright smile.

"Question. Can I take one of Missy's ribbons for that?" Astrid asked, lifting a hand.

I laughed. "I didn't come up with this, so Missy's comment wasn't about me. Let's say the game starts . . . now."

"I have a good story!" Vienna announced, sitting forward and grabbing a chip. "Remember last spring when London tried to take the train to Boston and ended up in Maine?" She pointed at London with her chip.

"'Omigod! Is this whole state populated by scary bearded men?'" they recited in unison.

Then they cracked up, laughing all over each other.

"That was one hell of a road trip coming to get you, though," Tiffany said, reaching for the M&M's. "The bathroom at the BP on 95?"

"Ew!" Rose groaned. "I dry-heaved for like an hour."

"Okay, I'm confused," Noelle said, raising a hand. "Is that a disparaging story about London's total lack of travel skills, or a funny anecdote about a road trip?"

"Give me a pin!" Ivy said, reaching a palm toward Noelle.

"What? No way," Noelle said firmly.

"No one said anything disparaging until you mentioned London's total lack of travel skills," Ivy countered. "Shocking that you were the first to insult someone."

"Okay, now you give me a pin," Noelle replied haughtily.

"What? Why?" Ivy said incredulously.

"Oh, I don't know. Maybe because you just insulted me to my face?" Noelle replied, crossing her arms over her chest.

I watched them face off and held my breath. This was supposed to be fun, not a showdown between Ivy and Noelle.

"Okay! Okay! That one's a wash," I said. "Let's move on."

Ivy and Noelle both rolled their eyes. Ivy reached for a peanut butter cup and Noelle shifted in her seat, turning her knees away from

Ivy and resting her arm on the back of the couch so that her back was practically square with Ivy's face.

"Anyone else have a story?" I asked, trying to break the uncomfortable silence.

"What about the time we all had to dress up Reed for her date with Hunter Braden!" Constance trilled.

"Oh! That was fun!" Portia put in, crunching into a pretzel.

"And necessary, considering your serious wardrobe issues," Missy said with a sniff.

"Now I definitely get your pin!" Astrid said.

"Oooooh!"

Missy rolled her eyes and detached a pin for Astrid. "Brown's not my color anyway."

As everyone started to reminisce about my makeover night last semester, studiously avoiding Sabine's name, I noticed, I began to finally relax. They were really getting into the spirit of the game—a game that Elizabeth Williams had devised almost a hundred years ago. Everyone was happy and laughing and shouting and pointing, grabbing pins from one another and chowing down. If I could just keep Ivy and Noelle from clawing each other's eyes out, everything would be fine. Because this was what I wanted the Billings Literary Society to be about. It was the closest we'd come to a true Billings moment since we'd returned from break.

And from that moment on, I vowed there would be many more.

CLOSE ENCOUNTERS

"Last night was so much fun!" Constance whispered as she slipped into the chair next to mine at breakfast the next day. "Was that the second task, or was it just for the heck of it? Because if it was a task, I guess Missy and Shelby totally failed."

"Shhh!" I said, glancing around to make sure no one was in earshot. Across the aisle, Gage, Sawyer, Graham, and Trey were hanging out, talking loudly. I ducked my head toward hers. "It was a task," I whispered. "And yeah, Missy and Shelby did not pass."

They had both lost all five of their pins quickly, but we'd decided to keep playing anyway. No one had wanted our night to end just then.

I speared some scrambled egg with my fork as Kiki, Vienna, London, Amberly, Tiffany, and the others settled in around us. Everyone was chatting, laughing, happy. After the first task I'd felt like we were prepping for a funeral. Now everyone was acting like we were on our way to the Legacy.

Not that I ever wanted to attend a Legacy party again after the awfulness of the last two, but still.

"We're going to movie night in the Great Room tonight," Vienna announced, laying her linen napkin across her lap. "They're showing a *Legally Blonde* marathon. Who's in?"

"Me!" London said predictably, lifting a hand. "I can recite the entire first movie from beginning to end."

But she couldn't get more than two answers right on the BLS knowledge test. Good to know she remembered the truly important stuff.

"Let's all go," Lorna enthused, dropping into her chair. "It'll be fun."

"Could be slightly more entertaining than my trig homework," Astrid mused, lifting a shoulder.

"I'm in," I said. I knew I should probably should spend the night studying, but I was happy that my friends wanted to do something together. This was what the secret society was all about—making sure we stayed close. It seemed like last night's loyalty message had come through loud and clear.

"Well, I, for one, don't need to spend the night watching Reese Witherspoon's career slowly wither and die," Noelle said with a sniff, carefully buttering her toast. "If any of you has progressed past a sixth-grade level, I'll be having a little soiree in my room."

Vienna and London drooped like they were a pair of puppies whose owner had just swatted their noses. My fingers clenched into fists under the table. Why did Noelle feel the need to make

everyone feel so inferior all the time? I opened my mouth to say
something when, much to the surprise of everyone at the table,
London spoke up.

"You don't have to insult us, Noelle," she said clearly, though not
making eye contact. "If you don't want to come, just don't come."

Vienna's jaw dropped.

"She's right," Rose said quietly. "We don't mock you for thinking
champagne and chocolate are the only gateways to a good time."

I had to look away. If I hadn't looked away, I would have laughed
out loud, which wouldn't have been very BLS of me. I had never heard
anyone other than myself or Ariana contradict Noelle. It was a historical moment.

Was I wrong to hope that the BLS had something to do with it?

"Fine. But I'll be there if anyone wants to join me," Noelle said.
Her tone was as confident as ever, but the words were somehow lack-
ing. Rose and London had gotten to her. Rose Sakowitz and London
Simmons, putting it to Noelle Lange. Maybe Mr. Hathaway was right.
Maybe things *were* on a more even keel this semester.

I was happily pondering this new development when the doors to
the dining hall opened and Ivy and Josh walked in together. My heart
lurched, as always. They made their way slowly toward us, glancing
over at the guys across the aisle like they were thinking about joining
them. Graham visibly stiffened. Josh paused and whispered something to Ivy, and she whispered something back, her eyes imploring.

This was intriguing. Finally, Ivy tugged Josh over to the table.
"Hey, guys," she said.

"Annoying couple." Gage greeted them with a laugh.

"Ha ha," Josh said uncomfortably. "Move in," he said to Trey.

Trey scooted his chair forward, but the second he did, Graham stood up from the table, shoving his chair back with a screech. Sawyer's face went ashen as Graham grabbed his bag.

"I'm done here," he said, sliding out past Gage's back.

He paused next to Ivy. "Hey," he said.

"Hey," she replied, looking at Josh in confusion. "You don't have to leave."

"Yeah. I kind of think I do." Graham shot Josh a look of death, then cleared his throat. "Excuse me."

Then he walked out of the cafeteria without looking back. Ivy shrugged and Josh sat down next to Sawyer, who shifted uncomfortably in his seat. Ivy took the vacated seat next to Gage.

"Okay. What was *that* all about?" Tiffany asked me.

"I have no idea," I replied.

Sawyer was getting up from the table now, moving sideways to get past Trey. Josh slumped further in his seat, clearly upset and embarrassed. What the hell was going on between Graham and Josh? I had been meaning to ask Sawyer, but I'd been so occupied with the BLS it had slipped my mind.

"Hey, Reed," Sawyer said, shouldering his messenger bag as he stopped at the end of our table.

"Hey," I replied.

From the corner of my eye I saw Constance and Tiffany exchange an intrigued look. My heart fluttered nervously. Great. Now I was going to have to endure a grilling about Sawyer and me. Couldn't a girl talk to a guy anymore without it being a crush thing?

"I was just going—" I said.

"I have to ask you something," he said at the exact same time.

I laughed and Sawyer blushed and looked at his feet. "You first," he said, his blond bangs falling over his face.

"No. You came to me," I said, turning in my seat to face him better. "You first."

"It's okay. You," he said.

I laughed. "Dude, just talk," I said, taking a bite of my bacon. "What's up?"

He pushed his hands into the pockets of his dark blue pants and puffed out his cheeks like a chipmunk. "I know it's kind of late notice, but . . . would you want to maybe go to the dance with me on Saturday?"

Tiffany sat up straight. Constance tensed beside me. Everyone at the table was watching us. Some, like Kiki and Shelby, were pretending they weren't by hiding behind their *Rolling Stone* magazine or scrolling along on their iPhone, but they *so* were.

"Um . . ."

I glanced past him at Josh and Ivy. They were holding hands across the table, leaning forward, talking in low tones as Trey and Gage fired up some game on their PSPs. Were those two ever *not* touching each other?

Time to move on, Reed. Get over it. Get a life.

Sawyer was nice. And a good listener. A good friend. Not to mention unbearably cute. And the guy had saved my life when I'd been about to drown in the Caribbean Sea. Besides, this wasn't necessarily a *date*, date, right? We could be going as just friends. Except one look at Sawyer's face told me that wasn't how he was looking at this. Somewhere along the line he had started to think of me as more than friend.

Could I think of him that way? I wasn't entirely sure.

Over at his table, Josh was now taunting Ivy with some eggs Benedict. She was squealing and shoving a warning finger in his face and pushing him away. Disgustingly adorable.

I turned around more fully, putting them out of my line of vision. Out of sight, out of mind.

"Sure," I said finally, looking Sawyer in the eye. "I'd love to go to the dance with you."

"Great!" Sawyer brightened considerably. "Cool. So . . . what did you want to ask me?"

My already sagging spirits drooped lower. I couldn't exactly grill him about his brother's obsession with my ex without looking like I was obsessed with my ex too. Didn't seem like the right note to hit seconds after making our first date.

"I was going to ask you, too," I said, blurting the first thing that came to mind. "To the dance."

Sawyer's smile widened. "Really? That's so . . . yeah?"

"Yeah," I said, feeling somehow as if I'd just made a serious error in judgment.

Damn this stupid dining hall throwing everyone together all at

once. There were too many distractions and too much sensory over-
load to make a sound decision.

"Great. Okay." He pressed his hands together, smiling ador-
ably. "So I'll just come to Pemberly then on Saturday night. Around
seven?"

"Perfect," I said, swallowing against a dry throat.

As Sawyer walked away, I kept my back to my friends, wanting to
postpone the inevitable twenty questions as long as possible. Do you
like him? How did you guys meet? Are you totally over Josh, then?
What're you going to wear?

I could practically feel their anticipation bubbling up behind me
and dreaded every second of it, because I had no idea how to answer.
Did I like him? I had no idea. How did we meet? Couldn't remember. Was I totally over Josh? No. What was I going to wear? Probably
something borrowed from one of them.

Not exactly the stuff romance novels were made of. But I took a
breath, turned around, and submitted to the shrieks and squeals.
This week was all about sisterhood, right? Let them have their fun.

THE THIRD TEST

"Ew! Omigod! I just stepped on a dead thing!"

Shelby screeched and barreled into me at the center of the chapel, holding on to me for dear life. I'd requested all the potentials wear "manual labor attire." For Shelby, this meant Paper Denim jeans, a cashmere "sweatshirt," tan kitten heels, and pearls. There were dots of sweat across her otherwise perfect brow and her hair was coming loose from its bun. All very odd since I hadn't seen her do a shred of work since we'd gotten there two hours earlier. Each potential—well, everyone except Constance, who, for some reason, had yet to arrive—had been given a chore. Shelby's task had been to clear the cobwebs from the wall sconces and candelabras—all of which were still filthy.

"What is it? Omigod, what is it? Do I have rabies?"

Her fingernails dug into my skin through her work gloves *and* the thick fabric of my Penn State sweatshirt. Half the girls scurried away from the wall where Shelby had been "working," which in her world amounted to waving a feather duster in the vicinity of a wooden sconce. Astrid, however, heaved a sigh and tromped right over, scanning her flashlight along the seam where the wall met the floor.

"It's just a mouse," she said.

"Ewwwwww!" everyone cried.

"I've got it, I've got it." Astrid dumped some old salt packets out of a brown paper bag and used it as a glove to pick the dead mouse up by its tail.

"Ewwwwwww!" The moans came as she lifted the thing toward the garbage pail. She dumped it in with a thud, then tossed the bag as well and smacked her hands together.

"Done. Let's move on, shall we?" she said, flicking her black bangs off her forehead with a glittery purple fingernail. "We're really making some progress here."

Astrid had been working her tail off sweeping the floors. I'd always known the girl was cool, but it was nice to know she wasn't afraid of a little dirt. Or a dead rodent.

"No. No way. That's it. I'm outta here," Shelby said, finally releasing me and raising her hands. She peeled off her yellow vinyl gloves and gingerly tossed them on the pew Lorna and Missy were dusting and polishing.

"Shelby, you can't go," Portia said. She had a streak of dirt across her cheek and a broom in her hand. For the first time since I'd known her, all the gold necklaces she wore were tucked inside her collar and her T-shirt was rumpled. Her makeup, however, was still perfectly intact. "If you leave . . ."

She looked at me, a question in her eyes. I turned to Shelby.

"If you don't complete the three tasks, you can't be considered for membership," I said. Although, she'd already been at the bottom of the list anyway, what with her poor showing on loyalty night (she'd lost her five pins almost as fast as Missy had lost hers), and with tonight's nonperformance. Not that she needed to know that.

My words hung thick and dark in the air. No one moved. Everyone held their tongues and waited to see what Shelby would do. She lifted her chin and stared me down.

"That's just fine," she said, reaching back to release her thick, golden brown hair from its band. It tumbled over her shoulders quite dramatically. "I'm a Wordsworth, in case you haven't heard. And we don't *do* dead things."

Then she turned on her heel, grabbed her coat off the old rack near the door, and stormed out into the night. Portia dropped her broom and went after her, shouting her name. We all heard the words "don't need Billings" and "already got into Cornell" carried in on the wind. Then Portia returned, alone, and lifted her hands in abject defeat.

We were down to fourteen. Well, thirteen if you considered the fact that Constance had never even shown.

"Come on, everyone," I said. "Let's get back to work."

"Well. That was interesting," Ivy said, shuffling toward me with her dustpan and brush. She filled it up with cigarette butts and dumped it into the garbage. Girl was wearing a white V-neck sweater and black jeans, neither of which looked the worse for wear, even though she'd been working all night.

"I'm not surprised," I whispered in response. "I've never seen Shelby with a fleck of lint on her person, let alone dust. And I figured some of the seniors would be out."

"Yeah, but I thought Noelle would be the first to go," she said, looking up toward the sky.

Noelle was right where she'd been since she'd arrived, up at the top of a rickety old ladder, working the grime off the stained-glass windows, alone. Part of me had to agree with Ivy. Who would have thought that Noelle would allow me, Glass-Licker, to put her through chore night at the old chapel? Especially when she hadn't wanted anything to do with the BLS to begin with? But then there was the other part of me. The part that knew that she was doing it just to prove to me that I couldn't faze her.

What I couldn't believe was that Constance hadn't shown up. Hadn't even called me to let me know. I'd tried her cell twice since we'd been there, but she hadn't picked up. The more time went by, the more concerned I grew. Could she be out there in the woods somewhere, lost? Each time I thought about it, I gave an involuntary shudder. Everyone was supposed to come in pairs. Constance was supposed to meet up with Lorna and they were to come together. But Lorna had waited and called and waited and called, and she hadn't wanted to get a black mark because of Constance's lateness, so she'd hooked up with Missy and Noelle and come with them.

Which was all well and good, but where the hell was Constance?

I glanced at the door. Nothing. I couldn't just stand around while everyone else was working, so I got back to the job of scraping gum from the floor, all the while keeping one eye on the entrance and one ear on the wind.

About an hour after Shelby made her dramatic exit, the chapel was looking habitable again. The pews had been dusted and polished to a shine. The floor was swept and scraped clean. The windows, though some were still broken, gleamed like crystal. Rose had finished polishing the pulpit and had offered to take on Shelby's job, so the sconces and candelabras were cobweb-free. The smells of rotting food and stale smoke had been replaced by the scents of evergreen and soapy water. I felt the ghosts of Billings Girls past smiling down on us with pride, and as I looked around at the tired but satisfied faces of the girls around me, I knew they could feel it too.

Aside from Shelby, most everyone had done their jobs, although I'd noticed that Lorna was putting in most of the work on the pews while Missy gabbed and moved a rag around halfheartedly. And London had spent half the night in the corner texting when she thought no one was looking. But as a group, we pretty much kicked ass.

"Can we get the hell out of here? My back is killing me," Noelle said, arching her back and shoving out her chest at the same time.

"Sure," I said with a smile. "But let's just take a second to pat ourselves on the back. Job well done, ladies."

I clapped my hands and everyone joined in, smiles all around. Then Lorna raised her hand.

"Yes, Lorna?" I asked.

"Just one question, Reed," she said. "Why did we just scrub down a condemned building in the middle of nowhere?"

"You'll know soon enough," I said, grinning from ear to ear and trying like hell not to make eye contact with Ivy.

For the first time in a while, I felt cheered by their groans. I was in charge and I liked it.

"Come on," I said. "I think we all deserve some serious sleep."

As we turned toward the door, it swung open with a bang. Every one of us froze.

Oh effing hell. I half expected Mr. Hathaway or my old buddy Detective Hauer to come storming through the door. If they were going to snag us, couldn't they have at least caught on *before* we killed ourselves working? But instead, Constance appeared. Her hat was askew, her face was red, and she clutched the doorknob, gasping for air.

"Did I miss it? Is it over? Oh my God, Reed! I'm so sorry!"

I rushed forward. Had Constance been lost in the woods all this time? Was she cold and wet and dehydrated? But when I got to her, Constance's skin was warm. Her eyes were bright and her feet were not soaked through.

"Are you okay?" I asked uncertainly.

"Yeah. Just, I basically sprinted up the hill trying to get here." Her eyes trailed over the crowd, all of whom were slowly pushing their arms into coat sleeves and yanking on their hats, their hair in various states of disarray, their clothes streaked with grime. Constance frowned. "Oh man. I really did miss it."

"Constance," I hissed, sensing that there was no tragedy to be related here. I pulled her away from the door. "Where have you been?

"I'm so sorry, Reed," Constance said. "It's just, Whit called and he's all freaking out about this chem assignment he has due tomorrow and if I don't talk him down he basically goes on a chocolate binge, which could send him into insulin shock and then he could end up in the hospital." She paused for breath. "Or dead!"

I felt sick to my stomach. She had missed the third task, after miserably failing the first, to talk to her boyfriend?

"Constance, you know there are only three tasks, right? This was the third," I said slowly.

"I know, but Reed! It was a matter of life and death!" Constance said. She looked around the chapel and her nose wrinkled. "What were you guys doing up here anyway? This place is horrible."

I wanted to wring her neck. Clearly she was not taking this seriously. At all. And on top of that, she was disparaging our chapel, the space we had all just worked so hard to clean. Without her help, I might add.

"Whittaker needs to learn to take care of himself," I told her. "You have to have your own priorities."

"I do!" Constance said, hugging herself. "It's just he's the first one. I mean, I love him. He's my first priority." Then she seemed to realize how serious I was and her face went slack. "I mean, no offense, Reed. Billings matters too of course! I really am sorry I didn't get here. Is there something I can do? Like a make-up test or something?"

A make-up test? Did this look like eighth-grade algebra to her?

"Are you guys coming or what?" Noelle asked, hovering at the door. Everyone else had already filed out.

"Yeah. We're coming," I said. I brushed by Constance, unable to look at her pleading eyes anymore, and headed out.

"Reed? Are you mad?" she asked, coming up behind me.

"No," I said, pulling my coat on as the cold hit me square in the chest. "I'm not mad."

Just disappointed. Because I knew now who one of the three cuts would have to be. And it was going to be devastating for both of us.

We trekked down the hill together, everyone laughing and whispering in the cold night air, going over Shelby's breakdown and Astrid's badass response. Tiffany, Portia, and Rose were quiet and subdued compared to the others, and I knew they were probably pissed off and disappointed that Shelby was out. I felt for them, losing their friend, but Shelby and I had never been close, and her leaving made the task ahead that much easier for me. Part of me was glad she'd gone on her own terms. It was better for her self-esteem and for my guilt.

As we reached the tree line we broke up into pairs, as planned, spreading out in the dark so that we'd all come onto campus at different spots, rather than in one huge clump. Ivy and I walked toward the east side of campus, Noelle and Missy behind us, Constance and Lorna behind them, ready to split again when we reached Parker.

"Hang on," Noelle said, right when Ivy and I were about to split off. "I'm going with our fearless leader. Ivy, you take Missy."

"Uh, since when do you tell me what to do?" Ivy asked.

"Does everything have to be an argument with you?" Noelle said, rolling her eyes. Then she paused and adopted a pious expression, placing her hands together at chin level. "Please, Miss Slade. May I please, please, please talk to Reed alone for a minute?"

The other girls laughed and looked away. Ivy turned red with fury and looked at me. "Reed?"

"It's fine. I'll catch up with you back at the dorm," I said.

"Fine. Let's go, Missy." She trudged off at lightning speed, and Missy almost slipped in the snow as she caught up.

I looked at Noelle, pretty much dying of curiosity over what she might have to say. "Well. That was obnoxious," I said.

She rolled her eyes again and turned down the hill toward campus, her footsteps crunching in the snow. "She'll get over it."

I sighed and jogged to catch up. No matter who held what positions of power, Noelle would always be Noelle.

"So, you're really getting the hang of this, Glass-Licker," she said, looking straight ahead as we walked. I bristled at the reemergence of the old nickname.

"The hang of what?" I said.

"Being the alpha girl." She ducked her head slightly, her hair falling across her face like a curtain. "I have to say I never thought I'd see the day Portia and Vienna got down on their knees and scrubbed a floor."

"They didn't go through Billings initiation like the rest of us?" I said.

She tossed her hair over her shoulder as she looked at me. "Let's just say the whole chore thing was slightly less intense before you came along."

"Oh."

Once again I got that acidic feeling in my gut. The feeling that I had been unworthy of Billings in the first place. That she was trying to remind me I'd never belonged.

"But seriously. Good job with all of this," Noelle said, our steps quickening as we reached the steepest part of the hill. "I wasn't sure you'd pull it off, but you did."

I inflated with pride so fast I thought I might go weightless. It was amazing, the effect she had on me. Putting me down one minute, puffing me up the next.

"Thanks." I grinned, feeling taller, lighter, happier. "I guess I did."

"You're gonna wanna stop right there."

Noelle and I froze. The male voice had come out of nowhere and scared every last gasp of breath right out of me. From behind the line of trees along Parker's north side, two security guards approached us, grins across their wind-dried faces.

"Come with us," the chubby one said, flicking his fingers. "The headmaster will see you now."

The skinnier one cackled and got behind us, as if we were going to try to make a break for it. Noelle's eyes met mine in the glow of one of the old-fashioned campus lights and the fury in them was enough to make me consider a sprint to the trees.

All Noelle had wanted to do was keep her head down and her nose clean, and graduate.

So much for that.

BLAME THE CAFFEINE

I expected to be dragged straight to Hell Hall, but instead, the security guards took us to the main chapel. Once again it was freezing inside, the space heaters having been dormant since that morning's services. Only the lights along the sides of the room had been illuminated, but I could see Headmaster Hathaway as clear as day, standing at the end of the aisle in the same suit and tie he'd been wearing on campus that afternoon. He wore a grim expression as we arrived at the front of the room. London, Vienna, Amberly, and Portia were already there, their expressions tense.

"Take a seat," Headmaster Hathaway said, gesturing at the pew across the aisle from our friends.

My butt hadn't even hit the hardwood when the door slammed again. We all turned around to find Lorna, Ivy, Missy, and Constance being ushered in by two more guards.

"Isn't this interesting?" Headmaster Hathaway said, eyeing them as they stepped tentatively toward us. "Tell me. Will anyone else be joining us?"

He looked at me briefly, but I wasn't about to say anything. At the back of the room, a direct-connect phone bleeped. There was an intelligible crackle of words. One of the guards replied to whatever had been said, then cleared his throat.

"The rest of the campus is quiet, sir."

I tried not to smile. That meant that Rose, Tiffany, Astrid, and Kiki had gotten back to their dorms without getting caught. I should award them extra BLS points for that feat.

"All right then. We'll have to deal with the people we have here," he said, looking down at Noelle and me as the latecomers slipped into the pew behind ours. "So. A literary society?" he said, crossing his arms over his chest and drawing himself up to full height.

Again, no one said a word.

"It's hard not to notice that this literary society is almost entirely made up of students who used to reside in the now defunct Billings House," he said, glancing back at the four security guards who now hovered behind us. "Is it not?"

"Yes, sir," the chubby guard answered. "I mean . . . no, sir? Is that a double negative?"

The smirk fell from Hathaway's face. "Tell me, Reed, what kind of literary society meets off campus, in the middle of a Friday night, in the dead of winter?" He quickly checked his watch. "Excuse me. It's now Saturday morning. Hmm?"

I gazed up at him, my lips pressed firmly together. This was one of

the suggestions the book contained on how to deal with authority figures when caught in an unexplainable situation. Say nothing, admit
nothing. He leaned one hand into the back of the pew, right next to
my face, and glared down at me. His tie swung forward, almost hitting
me in the nose.

"You're going to want to help me out, here," he said, so close I
could see the flecks of gold in his eyes. "Where were you all tonight?
What were you doing out there?"

My underarms prickled under the intensity of his gaze. I felt hot
from the tips of my toes to the tips of my ears. It was possible, that if
my friends hadn't been there, that if I hadn't propped myself up as
their leader, that if Noelle hadn't been sitting right next to me, as still
and strong as stone, I might have caved. But under the circumstances,
there was no way I could do that.

He turned his head and looked at Noelle. With his cheek in my
face, I could see the beginnings of a five o'clock shadow. Either he
wasn't very manly or he'd shaved twice today.

"Noelle? Anything you'd like to say?" he asked, standing up straight
again, smoothing his tie and stepping in front of her. "If I'm going to
call all of your parents in the middle of the night to report this infrac-
tion, they're going to want to know what you were doing out there."

Behind me, Constance let out a short whimper. Noelle shifted in
her seat, lifting one arm up to rest on the pew behind her and turning
her knees toward me.

"Honestly, Spencer, we couldn't sleep," she said, lifting her hand
to fluff her hair.

Mr. Hathaway's right eye twitched at the use of his first name, but he said nothing. Their families were, after all, friends. She'd been calling him "Spencer" her entire life.

"You really should think about shutting down that Coffee Carma," Noelle continued. "The caffeine is just awful for our still developing bodies."

Amberly squirmed behind us but, to her credit, said nothing about the potential closing of her father's business on campus.

"I appreciate your suggestion," Mr. Hathaway said sternly. "But it still doesn't explain what you girls were doing off campus in the middle of the night."

"We went for a walk," Noelle said. "I've heard exercise is one of the best ways to kill a caffeine buzz. And it definitely worked. I know I'm feeling very sleepy right about now."

She yawned and stretched her arms over her head, smacking the back of my head in the process.

"Me too," I piped in, loving Noelle in that moment. "What about you ladies?" I asked, looking around.

"Oh, definitely," Vienna said, faking a yawn.

Portia stretched her arms out at her sides while everyone else murmured their agreement, throwing in a few sighs and yawns and tired moans for good measure. Finally, I took a huge risk and stood up.

"If you don't mind, Headmaster Hathaway, we'd like to go back to our rooms now," I said. "I know *my* dad would hate to hear that we were kept out later than we needed to be so we could be grilled in an ice-cold chapel."

Mr. Hathaway eyed me with disappointment and disdain, but he backed away.

"Fine. These men will escort you back to your dorms."

My friends quickly roused themselves and we started down the aisle in a tense, quiet clump.

"Oh, girls?" Headmaster Hathaway said.

My eyes met Noelle's as we all turned around.

"Don't think for a minute that this is over," he said, stepping toward us. He gave us that grin—the one that was supposed to say that he was a down guy. The BFF of headmasters. Although right then, it clearly meant the exact opposite. "If I find out that you ladies are trying to re-form Billings House in some way . . . if I hear even a whisper about you asking for room transfers so you can be together or talking to the alumni or forming any sort of Billings club, I *will* be calling your parents, and I *will* be requiring their presence in my office as I conduct a disciplinary review for each and every one of you. Is that understood?"

Everyone nodded. Even me. Sudden, overwhelming fear had taken control of all bodily functions.

"Good," he said. "From here on out, I've got my eyes on you."

IN OR OUT?

If Mr. Hathaway thought we were all going back to our dorms to lie in our beds awake all night, fretting about what was to come, he was wrong. At least about me. I was up all night, but at my desk. The book was open in front of me, as well as all the notes I'd made during the last three tests. It was time to make my decisions. Which ten girls would make the cut, and which four would be out?

Some of the yeses were obvious. Tiffany, Rose, Ivy, Astrid, Kiki. All of them had aced the knowledge test, performed admirably on loyalty night, and worked the hardest on work night. Some of the nos were just as obvious. Shelby, who'd quit on her own, and, unfortunately, Constance.

Constance. My heart squeezed so tightly I thought I might actually cry as I wrote her name in the "no" column. This was going to crush her. But while everyone had done fairly well on loyalty night, Constance had had the worst score on knowledge night and hadn't even shown up for the final test. Going by the book, Constance would have to be deemed unworthy of membership in the Billings Literary Society. And if I was completely honest, I had to agree. She had blown off the third test to have a phone conversation with her boyfriend. A conversation she could have had before or after our gathering. Hell, if she had come to the chapel on time and told me what was up, I wouldn't have minded if she talked to him for a few minutes while working. But she hadn't done any of that. Billings was not a priority for her.

That awful decision made, I slowly went over the rest of the list. For a long moment, my pen hovered over Noelle's name. Going by the book, she was in. She'd gone five for five on knowledge night, done exactly as she was told on loyalty night, and finished her chore completely on work night. But still, I had to wonder, why was she really there? She had been so adamantly against it when I'd brought the idea to her in the first place. Had she only joined so that when she got tapped she could throw it right back in my face?

But then . . . she'd kind of saved our asses tonight, coming up with that silly but distracting story. And she had one of the highest scores when it came to the three tasks. I'd promised Ivy I'd go by the book, and that meant accepting Noelle.

Ironic that it was loyalty to a promise with Ivy that put her sworn enemy in the "yes" column. I wrote Noelle's name down, hoping I was doing the right thing.

Now it was clear to me who the final two cuts would have to be. One of them hurt. The other not so much. But I knew there would be dissension in the ranks when the final membership was revealed. I was just going to have to deal with that when it happened. They all knew there could be only eleven members. They all knew that fifteen of us had started the process. Four were going to have to go.

With a heavy but excited heart, I drew the first square of ivory stationery toward me and began to carefully write out my taps.

HARMLESS FLIRTING

Saturday morning dawned sunny and bright, and as I walked out onto the quad I was surprised by the warmth of the morning air. It was much less frigid than it had been since I'd returned to Easton, and I loosened my scarf to let my skin breathe, slowing my steps to enjoy the beautiful day.

Tucked deep inside my messenger bag were the eleven taps, including one for me. My heart fluttered with nervous excitement every time I thought about the huge step I was about to take. The hard part was over—the testing, the choosing. Very soon, the real fun would begin.

A sudden shriek sent my already alert nerves into panic mode and I whirled around. Ivy was out on the quad, wearing runners' tights and a down jacket, and she was being attacked via snowball by some guy I'd never seen before. He had spiked hair, a black leather jacket, and some kind of red and yellow tattoo on his neck. Definitely not an

Easton boy. As I stood there, frozen in place, Ivy bent to the ground and scooped up a snowball to retaliate, flinging it back at him with a shout. Tattoo Guy packed a mound of snow together and ran at Ivy with it, sending her shrieking and running toward the steps of Hell Hall. He grabbed her around the waist, shoving some of the snow down the back of her jacket, and she screamed, laughing and batting him away. As she turned around in his arms to face him, a fistful of snow in her glove, my heart all but stopped and I instinctively ducked behind the thickest tree I could find.

They were going to kiss. Oh my God, they were going to kiss! What the hell was Ivy doing?

Holy crap. What if she was cheating on Josh?

I peeked my head around the side of the tree. Ivy and Tattoo Guy were still staring into each other's eyes. They were far enough away that I couldn't read their expressions, but I could tell by his body language that the guy had a thing for Ivy, and from the suspended intensity of the moment, I had to assume that Ivy was attracted to Tattoo Guy, too.

Then, finally, she shoved the snow right in his face and ran off. The guy gave chase, grabbing up a skateboard I hadn't noticed before as he ran. A skateboard. Could this be one of the friends from Boston Ivy had told me about? Had he driven down to visit her? It was pretty early in the morning. If he'd done that, he would have had to have been up at the crack of dawn. But people did occasionally do that kind of thing. For love. Before Tattoo Guy could get anywhere near Ivy, she was safely slamming the door of Pemberly in his face with a laugh.

I leaned back against the trunk of the tree and took a deep breath.

My heart was racing as if I was the one who'd just been engaged in a flirtatious snowball fight. Ivy and Tattoo Guy flirting. Was he an ex-boyfriend or something? Did she want to get back together with him? Was she going to break up with Josh? And if any of these conjectures were even close to the truth, why hadn't she said a word about any of it to me? We'd been spending half our time together and we were supposed to be friends. Why would Tattoo Guy go unmentioned?

Speak of the devil: Tattoo Guy jumped on his skateboard and raced right past my tree, his wheels making a jarring racket on the cobblestones, knocking me out of my stupor. No. I couldn't think this way. Everyone flirted now and then. Everyone had off-campus friends. It didn't mean they were about to dump their boyfriends. Josh and Ivy were together. End of story. And tonight, I had a date with Sawyer.

LUDDITES

I slipped the taps into the mail slot and took a step back, taking a moment to myself to revel in my accomplishment. They'd said I couldn't bring Billings back from the dead, but I had. In a big way. I was honoring the women who had founded the sisterhood. Ushering us back to the old traditions and values and rituals. Being a Billings Girl was going to mean something again. Something more than being the wealthiest, the prettiest, the most powerful girls on campus. The sisters of the Billings Literary Society were going to make a difference.

I hadn't figured out exactly how yet, but I would. We would. Together.

"Good morning, Reed."

I whirled around. Headmaster Hathaway stood before me, his dark wool coat buttoned, his hands hidden under thick leather gloves. Where the hell had he come from—and how had he done it so silently? He stood so close that I backed into the wall to put a more comfortable distance between us. He, however, didn't budge. I glanced left and right, but the post office was deserted.

"I'm surprised to see you up so early," he said, tugging on the hem of his glove. "After our encounter this morning, I would have thought all you girls would be sleeping in."

"I've always been a morning person," I said, sliding away from him into the open area of the long, narrow room.

"Me too," he said. "I find there's nothing more invigorating than an early morning walk. It clears my mind. Makes me see things in a whole new light."

I swallowed hard and glanced at the mail slot. His eyes followed mine.

"For a girl of the Internet age, you certainly spend a lot of time in the snail mail office," he said with a joking grin.

"Yeah, well, my parents are Luddites," I told him. "They just can't seem to get the hang of e-mail. So I write to them at least once a week."

I was getting so good at the lying, I was starting to freak myself out a bit.

"Well, perhaps over spring break you should spend some time tutoring them," he said, stepping toward me. "Bring them up to speed with the rest of us."

"Yeah. Maybe," I said.

He hovered there for a moment, looking down at me as if he could somehow search inside my soul. Then, finally, his face broke into that casual Graham-esque smile he'd worn so often when we were in St. Barths.

"I'd like to make something clear," he said, taking a few steps toward the door, but turning back to look at me. "I know you're friends with Graham and Sawyer, and I appreciate your helping them acclimate to their new school, but I was serious about what I said last night. I may have a softer hand than Mr. Cromwell, but that doesn't mean I won't be putting a stop to illicit behavior, and I never, ever play favorites."

He tugged at the edges of his gloves again, then kneaded the palm of one hand with his thumb.

"Do I make myself clear?"

"Clear as day, sir," I replied, trying not to show my fear.

His eyes flicked to the mail slot again, and the smile was back. "Have a good day, Reed."

"You, too, Mr. Hathaway," I replied.

As the door swung shut behind him, dread spread through my chest like melting butter. He couldn't go through the mail, could he? What if he doubled back and found the taps as soon as I left the building?

But no. He'd need the key to get behind the counter, and only Lester the mail guy had that. Besides, wasn't tampering with the mail a federal offense or something? I took a breath and tried to shake off the creepiness of the encounter. Mr. Hathaway couldn't touch us. Not without proof, anyway. And so far, he had nothing but a niggling suspicion.

One thing was obvious, however. He'd been serious when he said he'd be keeping an eye on us.

ALL-POWERFUL

When I got the text from Suzel that afternoon, asking me to meet her in the solarium, I was surprised but also excited. I had suspected that she was the one who'd left the book for me, but her impromptu appearance on campus confirmed it. Now I was pretty much dying to talk to her about the whole thing. I couldn't wait to tell her that the tasks were already complete and that I'd sent out my taps. She was going to be so proud. And so glad that she'd picked me to carry on the Billings legacy.

By the time I arrived at the solarium, I was out of breath from the speed walk across campus. The bright, airy room was jam-packed with students and the noise level was at an all-time high. I shed my coat and scanned the room for Suzel, rising up on my tiptoes to see over the crowds of laughing guys and huddles of gossiping girls.

"Hey, Reed."

The sound warmed me from the inside out. Josh had just stood up from the table right next to me and now stood so close our knees would have touched if I'd shifted my weight. He pushed his hands into the pockets of his jeans and smiled slightly.

"What's up?" he asked.

"Um, nothing," I replied. I glanced at his table. He was alone, an AP biology textbook open in front of his chair. No Ivy in sight. Was that why he was finally initiating a conversation? "What's up with you?"

"Nothing." He reached behind him and scratched at the back of his neck. "How've you been? I've been meaning to call you. . . . I heard about St. Barths. . . ."

For the first time I forced myself to look into his eyes. Now? He was going to do this now? After all these days had passed? These weeks? Suddenly he cared that I'd almost died?

Something caught my eye over his shoulder. It was Suzel, lifting her hand. She was sitting on one of the settees over by the windows, wearing a crisp black suit with a pencil skirt.

"I'm sorry. I'm kind of meeting someone," I said. "I'll . . . see you around, I guess."

"Oh. Yeah. Okay," he said, his eyes darting around as if he was embarrassed.

Then he stood aside so I could pass him by. As I waved merrily at Suzel, she responded with a curt raise of a hand and an unpleasant pursing of lips.

Right. Okay. If I'd known she was going to shoot me that look, I might have taken my time getting over here.

I wove my way through the crowd, giving Tiffany and Rose a nod,

but passing them by. As I sat down at the opposite end of Suzel's set-
tee, I tried to shrug off the strange encounter with Josh, half wishing
I'd stayed behind to talk to him. I dropped my bag on the floor and
folded my coat in my lap.

"Hi, Suzel. It's good to see you," I said.

"Reed," she replied coolly. Her short blond hair was perfectly
coiffed and her lips perfectly outlined and glossy red. "Would you like
anything to drink or eat?"

"No, thank you."

"Good. Then I'll get straight to the point. Whatever you girls are
doing, it must stop, and it must stop now," she said quietly, almost
fiercely.

"What?" I asked, breathless. I felt as if my hair had been blown
back from my face.

"Look, Reed, the Billings alumni committee is working hard to get
Billings House officially reestablished," she said, flipping her hair
away from her chin. She sat up straight and smoothed her already
perfectly smooth pencil skirt with both hands. I wasn't used to this
all-business Suzel. Usually she was all bright smiles and laughter,
flashing her perfectly straight white teeth all over the place. "But if
that's going to happen, you and the rest of the girls are going to have to
quit sneaking around campus and start acting like the model students
we know you can be. Do you understand me?"

My brain felt all muddled and fuzzy. Like someone had just zapped
it with twenty volts of electricity. Apparently Suzel had not been the
alumna who'd left me the book. But if not her, than who?

"How did you even—"

"I've been reinstated to the Easton board of directors, and at our meeting yesterday afternoon, Headmaster Hathaway mentioned that there was a situation involving you girls that he was keeping a close watch on," Suzel said. "This morning he called me to alert me to the fact that several of you, along with Ivy Slade, were caught sneaking back onto campus in the dead of night from places unknown."

"But we were just following—"

Suzel lifted both hands to stop me. "The less I know, the better."

I couldn't live with that. Hadn't the note that came with the book been signed *Your sisters in BLS*? Sisters. Plural.

"Suzel, I'm only doing this because someone out there wants me to," I said. "Someone left the book for me and I'm just following directions."

Suzel's overly plucked eyebrows came together over her nose. She looked legitimately confused, as if I'd just started talking backward.

"What are you talking about? What book?" she asked. "Whose directions?"

The back of my neck prickled with heat.

Suzel did not know about the book. All-powerful, in-the-know Suzel. The one who had delivered my president's gift to me after I'd been elected—the designer purse and the wad of cash and the disc full of every bit of information ever gathered on all the Billings Girls present and past. The one who had directed us to the secret tunnel under Gwendolyn Hall so we could sneak off campus for the Legacy.

She clearly knew nothing about the BLS, the book, or the person who'd left it for me.

It was about time I stopped talking.

"Reed? What the hell is going on?" Suzel said, flipping from curious to concerned.

"I think you're right," I told her, gathering up my coat. "I think the less you know the better."

A flash of anger crossed her face as I stood. She reached out and grabbed my wrist. "Reed," she said through her teeth, "the reestablishment of Billings House is the alumni committee's number one priority. It's going to take time, but we will have the house rebuilt. We will return Billings to its former place of prestige. If you and your little friends decide to stand in our way, or do anything to threaten the accomplishment of this goal, the consequences will be dire."

My heart stopped beating. I knew how powerful the women on the alumni committee were. I knew that they could make or break all of us with a snap of their fingers. They were the women who were supposed to help us get into the Ivy League schools and land us prestigious internships and usher us into our future fabulous careers—or completely ignore us from the moment we graduated. But I also knew that someone had left that book for me. That they wanted me to do exactly what I'd done—what I was still doing. Someone far more powerful than Susan Llewellyn. I had to believe that that person was watching over me. That she would protect me. Protect all of us.

"Thank you for the warning," I said. Then I looked coolly, steadily down at her fingers. "You can let go of me now."

She seemed startled, and quickly released me.

"See you around, Suzel."

I walked out of the solarium as she fought for composure, feeling quite strong, forward-thinking, *and* eloquent. The sisters of the BLS, whoever they were, whoever had left me the book, would be proud.

JEALOUSY

"You look really pretty tonight, Reed."

Sawyer's expression was so serious I almost laughed.

"You said that already," I joked, trying to lighten the mood. This was, after all, a party. A mandatory one, but still. The dance floor was packed with couples swaying back and forth to the slow song played by the band on the platform stage, and everyone seemed to be having a decent time. Everyone except my date, who had clearly taken some intensity pills before picking me up.

"I did?" he asked, blanching. His hands pressed into my back and I got the distinct feeling he was trying to wipe the sweat off his palms. Tiffany wasn't going to appreciate it when I returned her purple silk Badgley Mischka to her covered in his handprints.

"When you picked me up," I said.

"Oh. Sorry."

"Don't worry about it. I'm just kidding," I told him, my heart squeezing in sympathy. "It's not like it's something a person can get tired of hearing."

Sawyer let out a small laugh and seemed to relax ever so slightly. "Yeah. I guess."

It was just too bad I wasn't hearing it from the guy I wanted to be here with. My eyes trailed across the room and found Josh, who was hovering near the door with Trey and Gage. Ivy was on the other side of the room, talking to Headmaster Hathaway of all people, laughing as she selected an hors d'oeuvre from one of the passing trays. But then, I guessed this was Double H's get-to-know you dance. Apparently he was getting to know Ivy.

Would it be wrong of me to go ask Josh to dance? One little dance never hurt anyone, right? But even as the thought occurred to me I knew it was a bad idea. Not only would Sawyer and Ivy probably not appreciate the gesture, but it would be bad for my heart. Dancing with Josh would leave me with ten thousand questions and feelings I wasn't supposed to be having.

"Everything okay?" Sawyer asked.

I looked up at him and saw my friend. The sweet, stoic guy I'd gotten to know down in the Caribbean. Sawyer cared about me. Josh, on the other hand, hadn't called me on Christmas or when he'd heard I'd been rescued from several murder attempts and a week on a deserted island. He hadn't texted or e-mailed or called once since we'd been back and he'd barely said anything to me other than hello or good-bye. It was pretty clear which one of these guys deserved my attention.

I just wished I could feel the way about him that he was clearly starting to feel about me.

"Yeah," I said. "Everything's great."

I held him a little tighter and rested my cheek on his shoulder. It felt comfortable. Not exciting, but comfortable. Maybe I could live with comfortable. Not every relationship had to be all heart palpitations all the time, right? Perhaps it was better—safer—if they weren't. Sawyer adjusted his arms and I could feel his breath warm on my bare neck. As we turned in a slow circle, I almost tripped the both of us.

Josh was staring right at me. For the first time all night. It was as if he'd just realized I was there. Heart palpitation city. The moment he saw me looking he colored and looked away, but I could tell he was thrown. And suddenly I wanted to go over there and scream at him.

Seriously? That was all it took to get his attention? Putting my cheek on some guy's shoulder? Why hadn't I thought of that before?

"Hey, guys."

Graham joined us on the dance floor. I lifted my head and did a double take when I saw who his partner was. Dark hair in an elaborate bun at the nape of her neck. Green silk halter dress I'd helped pick out, silver Jimmy Choo heels.

"Hey, Ivy," I said, my brow knitting.

"Hi." She shot me a baffled look, like she wasn't sure how she'd ended up in this situation either—wrapping her arms around the neck of the guy who obviously hated her boyfriend.

Sawyer stopped dancing. "Graham. What're you doing?"

"Dancing," Graham said with a shrug, slipping his arm around

Ivy's waist. "Although I kind of suck at it. Maybe you shouldn't have said yes," he joked, looking down at Ivy.

"As long as I come out of it with all ten toes intact, we're good," she replied.

I glanced past them at Josh. He did not look happy.

Graham smiled and pulled Ivy closer, the emerald green silk of her dress catching on one of the buttons of his suit. Ivy's cheeks turned pink. I couldn't tell if she was embarrassed or pleased, but Josh had just put his empty cup down, his face flushed with anger.

"Uh, hey, Graham, you just met the girl," I joked.

He and Ivy just kept dancing as if they hadn't heard me. I looked at Sawyer. He was staring in the same direction I'd been staring half the night. At Josh. Who was quickly moving our way. Josh's jaw was set and he was so focused he barely noticed he was slamming into people as he barreled across the dance floor. I'd never seen Josh out for blood before.

It was hot.

But it wasn't for me.

"Graham," Sawyer said, putting his hand on his brother's arm. "I think you need to find someone else to dance with."

"Lighten up, Sawyer," Graham said. That was when Josh arrived.

"Hey, man," he said, stopping next to us. "Is that really necessary?"

Graham sighed and backed away from Ivy slightly, still holding on to her hand as he turned to face Josh.

"Back off, Hollis. She doesn't belong to you," Graham said.

"I don't belong to anyone, thanks," Ivy said, wresting her hand free.

A few couples near us took notice of the serious vibe and stopped dancing. My face grew warm and I glanced toward the group of teachers and administrators milling near the wall. How long before *they* started to notice?

"Hey. The song's not over," Graham said, reaching for her.

Josh slipped right between them and put his hand flat in the center of Graham's chest. Oh, fab. Physical contact had been made. It was all downhill from here. Someone in the crowd even let out an excited "ooooh!" The music continued to play, but fewer and fewer people were dancing to it.

"I think we're done here," Josh said, looking Graham in the eye.

Graham stared down at Josh's hand. "See, that's where you'd be wrong."

And then he pulled his fist back and slammed it into Josh's jaw. There was a sickening crack and then someone screamed. It might have even been me. I have no idea. The next two minutes were a blur of flailing arms, spurting blood, and scrambling couples. Suddenly Graham was on top of Josh on the floor and Ivy and Sawyer were trying to grab his arms. Josh's face was purple from the struggle and his temple kept slamming into the polished wood over and over and over again.

"Someone do something!" I shouted.

All of a sudden Mr. Hathaway and two security guards descended on the melee. It took all three plus Sawyer to drag Graham off Josh.

"Graham! Stop!" Headmaster Hathaway shouted, holding a hand up to Graham until he quit struggling against the guards.

Slowly, Josh pushed himself onto all fours. He spat a wad of blood onto the floor and one of the girls nearby let out an "ewwww." Ivy helped him get to his feet, where she gingerly touched his face with both hands, trying to assess the damage. Over her head, Josh's eyes found mine. He looked ashamed and scared and sorry and angry all at once. And somehow, I understood.

"Are you all right, son?" Mr. Hathaway asked.

Josh managed to nod, holding the back of his hand to his bleeding lip. He looked around at all of us—at Ivy, at me, at Sawyer, at the rest of the gaping crowd—and suddenly took off, jogging out the door into the hall. Ivy went after him, but she stopped at the doorway. My guess was Josh had already fled the building.

Mr. Hathaway turned to Graham. "You. In my office. Now."

Graham pulled down on his jacket and flicked his hair back from his face. I half expected him to crack a grin and somehow explain that this was all a joke, that none of that really just happened, but instead he sniffed and headed out the opposite door—the one that led directly outside and into the freezing night.

"I'm coming with you," Sawyer said to his father.

Sawyer. I'd nearly forgotten he was there.

"No. You stay," his father said curtly, sounding like he was ordering around a dog. He took a breath and let it out, then added in a more normal tone. "You and Reed have fun. Your brother and I need to have a little chat."

One of the members of the cleaning staff was already down on her hands and knees, cleaning up the blood. Slowly everyone was coming out of their stupor, starting to whisper and gossip and laugh.

"Reed! Are you okay?" Constance asked, emerging from the crowd with Walt Whittaker at her heels. He'd driven down from Harvard to escort Constance to our school soiree. I was offhandedly glad to know he was as there for Constance as she was for him. When she found out about the taps, she was going to need a shoulder to lean on.

"Yeah. I'm fine," I said, still shaken. My pulse was throbbing in my face, my ears, my tongue. I looked at Sawyer, who was staring at the blood smear slowly disappearing under the hypnotic circular motions of a white rag. "Sawyer, are *you* okay?"

"What?" he said, blinking. He touched a small scrape on his right cheek. "Oh yeah. I'm okay. I just got clipped by Graham's watch, but otherwise I'm good."

"Good. So tell me, what the hell is it with Josh and Graham?" I asked. "Clearly whatever it is, it's not good."

Sawyer's pale face slowly turned pink under the rotating disco ball. "It's not my story to tell," he said. "If you want to know, you're going to have to ask Graham."

Again with the secrecy. Couldn't anyone just give a straight answer around here? Then again, I'd been at Easton long enough to know that the answer to that question was no. Well, fine. If I had to talk to Graham, I would. I just hoped it was the Graham I'd known in St. Barths. Because this violent version of him might have been new, but it was definitely not improved.

HAPPY

It was a clear, frigid night, a blanket of stars winking overhead as we speed-walked toward the dorms after the dance. I held my coat closed at my throat and tried to pick out Ivy's window at the back of Pemberly. Jillian was behind me somewhere with her boyfriend, so that meant that if Ivy's light was on, she was home. I had to get to her. Had to find out what had happened with Josh. Find out whether he was okay. Whether Headmaster Hathaway had decided to discipline him. Who knew what kind of punishment our new headmaster would hand down for breaking up his get-to-know-you dance with a brawl?

"Hey, Reed? What's the rush?" Sawyer asked.

I slowed my steps and looked back at him. Ever since Graham and Josh had been tossed out of the dance, I'd been tense and worried and trying very hard to pretend I wasn't tense and worried. Sawyer, however, had seemed to finally relax. He'd been talkative, happy, and loose ever since his father, brother, and Josh had left the room. As if he could finally breathe without them there.

He caught up with me and slipped his hand into mine. My heart thumped extra hard. There was no denying it anymore—in Sawyer's eyes, we were on a real date. Our first date. And here I was stressing about my ex.

But there was nothing I could do about it. My brain, my heart, my soul were all preoccupied. I loved Josh. There. Simple as that. And love wasn't something that just went away if you wanted it to. And I wasn't even sure that I *did* want it to. Why should I? Just because he was with Ivy and Sawyer was clasping my hand? There was always a chance we could get back together. Was I horrible for hoping?

"So, that was fun," Sawyer said, swinging my hand slightly. "Except for the fight part."

"Yeah. That part was not good," I replied, looking down at my feet as we walked. The pace was slow and torturous. I was practically salivating to get back to the dorm. To find out what the hell was going on. "So . . . how do you like Easton so far?" I asked, needing to fill the silence.

"It's okay," he said, kicking a rock off the path and into the snow. "I've been to three private schools already and they're all pretty much the same. Musty books, ancient teachers, lots of talk of tradition."

"I can imagine," I said, scanning Pemberly again now that we were closer. I found Ivy's window next to mine. It was completely dark. My hopeful heart sank like a stone. Did that mean Josh was seriously hurt? What if he'd been whisked away to the hospital with Ivy at his side? The thought made my stomach turn.

"I'm glad we have a lot of classes together, though," Sawyer said with a smile.

Again my heart gave a sickening thump. He was trying to flirt. Why had I accepted this date? What was wrong with me? I should have known that he wanted to be more than friends. Why did I never see these things coming?

"Yeah. At least you knew a few people here before you started," I said, trying to make it like I was just one of many. "That must have made it easier."

"Definitely," Sawyer said.

We paused at the bottom of the steps to Pemberly. A few people coming up from behind slid around us and went inside. I saw a couple of senior girls glance back at us and knew they were gossiping either about our coupling or Sawyer's crazy-ass brother. Would tonight's antics be good for Graham's image around Easton, or bad?

"Well. This is my stop," I said.

This is my stop? How big of a dork was I? But then, maybe that was a good thing. Maybe he'd be turned off by my dorkitude.

"We should do it again sometime," Sawyer said, releasing my hand. "But something normal. Like dinner or something."

I swallowed the rocks in my throat. "Yeah. Um, maybe."

Sawyer took a step closer to me. He was going in for the kiss. A huge part of me wanted to turn away, but then I thought that maybe if I let him kiss me it would change everything. Maybe I'd suddenly feel this surge of attraction and I'd want to be with him as much as he clearly wanted to be with me. It would make everything so much easier. Sawyer and I could be together. Josh and Ivy could be together. Everyone could be happy. All I wanted was for everyone to be happy.

So I let Sawyer kiss me. A quick, flat kiss on the lips. It was like kissing my brother. Sawyer leaned back, stars in his eyes. He was blushing like mad and couldn't stop smiling.

Crappity crap.

"See you tomorrow?" he said, lifting his brows.

"Yeah. Sure," I replied.

Then I turned and trudged into my dorm as Sawyer practically skipped away.

DISAPPEARED

Josh wasn't at breakfast the next morning. Neither was Graham. And when I'd knocked on Ivy's door at six a.m. I'd woken a very cranky Jillian, who had told me Ivy hadn't come back to the dorm at all. So even though I was intimately connected to all the players, I was in the same position as every other gossiping soul in the dining hall—that of wondering what the hell was going on.

I should have been focused on that night's initiation. Should have been making sure everything was in place and finalizing my plans. Maybe even figuring out a way to soften the blow for those who hadn't been asked to join, because soon enough, they were going to figure it out. But instead all I could do was obsess about Josh.

And Ivy and Graham, too, of course.

"Do you think they got expelled?" Lorna asked, taking a bite of her bagel.

"The headmaster is not going to expel his own son," Noelle replied, flicking some invisible lint from her black sweater.

"Which is good, right?" Tiffany said. She pressed her forearms against the edge of the table as she leaned forward to better see the rest of us. "For Josh, I mean. You can't exactly expel one of them and not the other."

"There's no way he's expelling Josh," I said, trying to sound more confident than I felt. "He didn't even start it."

"Really? I heard he freaked when he saw Graham all over Ivy and that he threw the first punch," London said, her mouth full of fruit.

"No way. I was standing right there. Josh got in front of Graham to keep him away from Ivy, but Graham definitely punched first," I said.

Unless you counted the hand to the chest that Josh gave Graham, but I didn't. It wasn't even a shove. More of a stop sign.

"If you say so," Noelle said blithely, taking a sip of her juice.

"What's that supposed to mean?" I blurted.

"Just that you're not the most . . . *objective* observer when it comes to Josh Hollis, that's all," Noelle said.

"Oh no she didn't," Portia joked, eliciting laughter from everyone else at the table.

My already overwrought mind had started to formulate a seriously scathing response when there was a hiss of heightened noise across the dining hall. I looked up to find Ivy walking toward us. I jumped out of my seat, nearly knocking my chair over in the process, and elbowed Vienna in the head.

"Ow!"

"Sorry!" I blurted, tripping over myself on my way to meet Ivy in the aisle. Her long red coat was open over an ankle-length black skirt and gray top and her face was makeup free. She hugged me as soon as I got to her.

"Hey!" I said. "Are you all right? Where have you been?"

"I called my mom and she came and picked me up," Ivy explained. "I just kind of wanted to sleep in my own bed last night." She looked around the dining hall, the lights making her pale skin appear almost tissue thin. "Where's Josh?"

My heart sank like a stone. "I was hoping you knew. No one's seen him."

"What? Seriously?" Ivy said, her brow wrinkling. "Did you talk to Trey?"

"Yeah. Josh never came home last night either," I said. I was starting to wish I hadn't scarfed down all those Apple Jacks. My stomach was starting to revolt.

"So where the hell is he?" Ivy asked, whipping her cell phone out of her pocket. "I've been texting him all morning and he hasn't replied."

I swallowed my pride before saying the next thing that came to mind. "Have you tried his parents? Maybe he did the same thing you did."

She shook her head. "Called them on my way here. They said Double H called them about the fight and was going to keep them posted on the disciplinary action. That's all they know so far. They were kind of freaked, actually. According to his mom, Josh has never punched anyone in his life."

Which begged the question once again—why all the tension between Josh and Graham?

"What the hell did Hathaway do? Lock him in a dungeon some-where?" I asked, starting to feel desperate.

Ivy bit her lip. "I don't know. God, I'm such an idiot. If I hadn't said yes to Graham, this never would have happened."

"So why did you?" I asked.

"Well, his father was standing right there," she said defensively, raising a palm. "I couldn't shoot him down in front of his dad."

Someone dropped a glass and I looked around, remembering where we were. Almost every pair of eyes in the room was trained on Ivy and me. For the first time I noticed that Sawyer wasn't at his usual table either. My skin tingled with trepidation and uncertainty. What was up with the Hathaways? I'd thought Sawyer's dad was going to be a kinder, gentler headmaster, but he was turning out to be a huge enigma.

"I have an idea," I said, linking my arm through Ivy's and turning her around.

"Where're we going?" she asked.

"Double H is all about this open-door policy, right?" I said as we headed for the door. "I think now's the perfect time to take him up on it."

I grabbed my stuff and Ivy and I walked through the cafeteria, ignoring our audience. Ivy shoved open the door and I tugged my coat on as we speed-walked directly to Hell Hall. It was pretty quiet inside, what with the entire student body and most of the faculty back at the dining hall. As we jogged up the stairs to the headmaster's office, the only sounds were of someone tapping on a distant keyboard, and the whirring of a copy machine.

The door to the headmaster's outer office was, in fact, open, but there was nobody behind his assistant's desk. My old friend and informant, Miss Lewis, had left her post at this desk at the end of my sophomore year. I wasn't sure who was supposed to be manning it now, but whoever it was, he or she was on a break.

Ivy and I hesitated in the center of the thick rug. We could both hear Mr. Hathaway's muffled voice coming from the other side of the heavy wooden door on the far side of the room. Even though I felt a skitter of nerves, I walked purposefully over to the door and lifted my hand to knock.

That was when I heard him say, clear as day, "... no coincidence that it was all Billings Girls."

I froze. Ivy and I looked at one another, wide-eyed. Hathaway must have been pacing the room as he talked, because those few words were loud and precise, but his voice was already much further away and indistinguishable.

I held my breath and waited. If he was talking about us, I had to hear more.

"What are you doing? Knock!" Ivy whispered.

I shook my head. His voice was growing closer again.

"... know that. Of course. Well then perhaps we should make some calls. Some of the alumni would be interested to know, I'm sure. ..."

My eyes narrowed. Know what? Was he still talking about us? Who was he going to call.

"Oh, for God's sake," Ivy whispered.

She shoved me out of the way and lifted her fist to knock.

"Excuse me, ladies. Can I help you?"

We whirled around. An elderly woman with extremely short, gunmetal gray hair stood in the doorway, wearing a purple suit and clutching a folder. My heart was in my throat.

"Yes. We're here to talk to the headmaster," Ivy said.

The woman gave us a rueful smile as she crossed to her desk. "I'm afraid the headmaster is on the phone and asked not to be disturbed."

Ivy walked toward the desk. "But I thought he had an open door policy."

The woman sat primly and folded her hands in front of her, looking up at Ivy. "I'm sure you can appreciate that said policy cannot possibly be enacted at every moment of every day, miss. Now, if you like, I can set an appointment for you."

She pulled out her keyboard and hit a few buttons. "How does fourth period tomorrow strike you?"

Ivy looked like she knew exactly whom she wanted to strike.

"Forget it," I said, grabbing Ivy's arm. "We'll just come back later," I said.

"All right, then! Have a productive day, girls!" the woman called after us.

Ivy cursed under her breath as we tromped back down the stairs.

"Don't worry," I told her. "If Josh and Graham aren't in the chapel, we'll just corner Double H afterward and ask him what's going on."

"Fine," Ivy said. "Open door policy my ass."

Out on the quad everyone was headed toward the chapel. I tried to keep up with Ivy's frenzied speed-walking pace, but I my thoughts were all over the place and I had to slow down. Had to get a grip. Who was Headmaster Hathaway talking to and why was he talking about the Billings Girls? Which alumni was he going to talk to and about what? At the very center of the quad, a cold wind blew my hair forward over my face and I turned into it so it would send my thick mane back over my shoulders. Just then, Headmaster Hathaway walked out of Hell Hall and paused on the top step to tug his leather gloves over his hands. He was yards away, but he looked right into my eyes. And the chill that shuddered through me had nothing to do with the wind.

INITIATION

The Billings Literary Society might have been thorough in certain respects, but there was one important bit of information the original sisters had neglected to jot down:

Initiation was a bitch.

Technically, I was supposed to blindfold everyone and bring them up to the chapel in a line, each girl holding the shoulder of the girl in front of her —all of them dressed in head-to-toe white.

Yeah. Like Headmaster Hathaway and his goons weren't going to find that at all suspect. Figuring that the sisters of the BLS would understand my making some minor adjustments in order to keep our secret society a secret, I arranged for each of them to come to the door of chapel at a separate time, just as I'd done for our very first meeting. I was there when the first girl, Lorna, arrived, and I quickly blindfolded her at that point and tucked her away in the far corner of the chapel so that she wouldn't be able to see who else had made the cut until the big reveal moment.

One by one they emerged from the woods. Kiki, Astrid, Ivy, Vienna, Tiffany, Rose, Portia, and Amberly. As I blindfolded Amberly, she was quaking from either nerves or the cold and I tasted bile in the back of my throat. I couldn't believe that Amberly freaking Carmichael had gotten in to the BLS and not Constance. It was the first time I seriously, and on a deep, physical level, wished I had broken the rules. I stashed her in the deepest, darkest, coldest corner of the chapel and felt a teeny bit better when I heard her whimper.

Noelle was the last to arrive.

"What the hell do you think you're doing with that?" she said, leaning away from me as I approached with the blindfold.

I rolled my eyes. "Just shut up and trust me."

She rolled her eyes right back. "Fine. But don't mess up the hair."

I tied it extra tight, reveling in the involuntary squeak she let out as the blindfold tugged her tresses. As I took her hand and led her carefully up the crumbling steps, I glanced back at the trees to make sure no one had followed her. The woods were silent except for the rustling of the branches in the wind.

We were safe. At least for now.

Inside, I led Noelle down the broom-cleaned aisle and stood her right at the base of it, in the center of the open area before the pulpit. Then I quickly moved around the room, lighting each of the brand-new candles I had placed in the sconces and candelabras that afternoon. If Headmaster Hathaway was really keeping an eye on us, he'd fallen down on the job today. I'd been back and forth to the chapel three times getting everything set up and hadn't been bothered by a single guard or faculty member. Maybe Double II was just preoccupied with the fight between Graham and Josh and had forgotten all about the Billings Girls for the moment. I'd have to thank the guys for that later—if I ever saw them again.

Mr. Hathaway had fled the chapel after services so fast I wasn't even out of my seat by the time the doors had closed behind him. Ivy and I had stopped by his office again after first period, then after lunch, then after dinner, and each time we'd been turned away by his evil secretary.

No one saw Josh, Graham, or Sawyer all day long. It was as if they had all been snatched by aliens in the middle of the night. Every time I thought of Josh my heart seized with concern, but I had to put him out of my mind for the moment. Right now, I had to be here for my sisters.

Once all the candles were lit, I started to make my way around the chapel, nudging the girls from their secret spots and lining them up carefully next to Noelle. Their feet shuffled along unsteadily as I brought them from every corner and cranny of the chapel. I could tell they were growing impatient to find out what was going to happen next and I was right there with them. By the time I placed Amberly at the end of the line and took my spot at the pulpit in front of them, I was sweating through my black dress. I took a moment to breathe, and looked down at them, all lined up in their outfits of white, some of them sniffing the air as if they could get some idea of where I was. I imagined the first sisters of the BLS gathered inside the chapel. Imagined Elizabeth Williams facing her blindfolded friends just like I was doing right then, and my heart was full.

I opened the book on the podium in front of me, took a breath, and smiled. The room was aglow with the light of six dozen candles and filled with the scent of melting wax. Waiting atop the dividing wall between the pulpit area and the choir pews behind me were ten white candles and one black, the last for me. Much as in the Billings House initiations I'd been a part of, each of the initiates was going to receive a white candle, which I was to light with my black one. The wording used in the initiation was even the same. I wondered if anyone who had been initiated into Billings House over the last thirty years realized that the ceremony was based on this secret society stuff.

"Welcome, sisters, and congratulations. You have all been deemed worthy of membership in the Billings Literary Society. You may now remove your blindfolds."

Everyone whipped off their white cloths and looked around, blinking blearily. I held my breath as I waited for all of them to take in the group. To realize that Constance and London and Missy were not among them. Noelle frowned thoughtfully but didn't seem surprised. Vienna, however, was dumbfounded.

"Where the hell is London?" she blurted.

"Ladies, this is a solemn occasion. You are to remain silent until we take the vow of—"

"Screw that," Vienna said, stepping out of line. "How could you leave out London?"

"And Missy. She can't not be here," Lorna said shakily. "She's going to freak."

Everyone started to talk at once. I'd known they were going to be upset, but we were only two seconds in and I was already starting to lose control. I saw Noelle start to open her mouth to silence them and I brought both hands down on the sides of the podium, hard.

It did nothing.

I slammed the book closed, lifted it, and dropped its hefty weight into the surface of the podium. Everyone stopped talking.

"Get. Back. In. Line," I said through my teeth.

They hesitated for a moment, but then quickly re-formed a straight row. I took a deep breath to slow my adrenaline rush.

"You all knew from the very beginning that this society was going to have only eleven members," I said slowly, looking at each of them in turn. "The people in attendance here completed the three tasks admirably. Some of our friends . . ." I paused, my voice starting to crack as I thought about how crushed Constance was going to be. "Some of our friends did not perform as well."

Everyone stared at me. Total silence.

"From the beginning I've been honest with all of you. I'm going to conduct this secret society in the spirit in which it was originally founded," I told them. "That means adhering to a new level of sisterhood, loyalty, and excellence. The eleven of us who are gathered here are going to work hard, stick together, and have a lot of fun. But I need all of you to be one hundred percent in. If you're not—if you don't want to be a part of this—now's the time to leave."

I glanced at the door behind them. Vienna looked over her shoulder at it too. Then down at her feet. Then, ever so slowly, she lifted her chin and faced forward again. Lorna looked like she was going to barf, but she didn't move. Noelle stared down Ivy, who, much to her credit, kept her gaze dead ahead. If Noelle said something about how Ivy didn't belong there—about how she'd taken the spot of a true Billings Girl . . .

But she said nothing.

I took a deep breath and counted to ten. Then counted to ten again. I had my answer.

"Good," I said finally, smiling. "Now we can get started."

I turned and gathered up the ten white candles. Vienna completely avoided my gaze when I handed one to her. Lorna shifted from foot to foot, giving me a tentative glance, as if she wasn't entirely sure she was supposed to be there. Hopefully, by the end of this ceremony, they would both feel better about the society. I wanted everyone to be happy to be there. No reluctant members allowed.

I lit my black candle and quickly read over what I was supposed to say and do. Then, taking a nervous breath, I approached Noelle.

"Sister," I said, looking into her eyes, "state your name."

She smirked. "Noelle Lange."

"Noelle, please repeat after me," I said. "I, Noelle Lange."

"I, Noelle Lange."

"Do hereby vow to be loyal, steadfast, and true to the Billings Literary Society and to my sisters."

"Do hereby vow to be loyal, steadfast, and true to the Billings Literary Society and to my sisters."

I smiled and touched my flame to the wick of her candle. As the light flickered across her face, I recited the final, somewhat familiar line. "We welcome you, Noelle, to our circle."

She blinked in recognition. From the corner of my eye, I saw Tiffany, Vienna, and Rose exchange an intrigued glance. *That's right, ladies.* Our Billings House initiation trickled down from here. It all started with that book. I was happy they were finally starting to realize what it meant, why we were here. I moved on to Tiffany, who grinned as she repeated her promise.

Each of my friends recited their vows in turn. When I got to Vienna, she still wouldn't meet my eyes.

"Sister, state your name," I said.

"Vienna Clarke," she said in a bored tone, holding her candle at a careless angle.

My heart broke at the sight of her slumped posture, her annoyed vibe. I knew she was aching for London to be there even worse than I was aching for Constance. As I lit her candle, I realized I wouldn't be the least bit surprised if she came to me tomorrow and told me she was quitting. I so didn't want her to do that. She'd made it this far. To quit now, before we all decided what this society was really going to be about, would be such a shame.

Kiki recited her vow with her shoulders rolled back, her eyes serious. Then, as I touched my candle to hers and said, "We welcome you, Kiki, to our circle," her entire face lit up with the widest smile I'd ever seen. It was all I could do to keep from laughing out loud.

Lorna was next. I looked into her eyes. Her brow was knit with a question. I had a feeling she couldn't wrap her brain around the fact that she had made it in and Missy—the girl she'd been playing sidekick to for Lord knew how many years—had not. I wanted to just smack her upside the head and tell her she had worth on her own. That she had in fact scored higher than half the people here. She belonged here. I wanted her to believe it.

"*Sister*," I said pointedly, trying to emphasize the fact that this was her sisterhood as much as it was everyone else's, "state your name."

"Lorna Gross." Her voice was meek.

"Repeat after me. I, Lorna Gross." I stared into her eyes, trying to bolster her.

"I, Lorna Gross," she said, staring back.

"Do hereby vow to be loyal, steadfast, and true to the Billings Literary Society and *my* sisters," I said.

As Lorna repeated the words, her posture straightened considerably. "Do hereby vow to be loyal, steadfast, and true to the Billings Literary Society and *my* sisters."

She grinned, and I grinned back.

"We welcome you, Lorna, to our circle."

"Thanks, Reed," she blurted.

Everyone giggled and Lorna turned red, but I just smiled and moved on.

After that, initiating Amberly wasn't quite as painful as I'd imagined it would be. And then, we were done. All eleven of us stood there in the drafty old Billings Chapel, our candles flickering in the darkness, our faces illuminated by the common light of our sisterhood. As I looked at their eager, expectant faces, my heart swelled and I suddenly decided to break from script. Just for one moment. I stood at the center of the semicircle and held out my candle like a glass of champagne.

"To Billings," I said.

Nine of the ten of them raised their candles as well. And I couldn't exactly blame Ivy for not joining the toast. She knew I was talking about the house the rest of us had so recently lost, and not about our new sisterhood. But still. I felt it needed to be done.

"To Billings!"

NOT HER

I couldn't sleep. I kept running over the initiation ceremony again and again in my mind, how we'd all hugged and celebrated when it was over, the giddy whispers and laughter echoing through the trees as we traipsed through the snow down the hill toward campus.

This was the biggest, most important thing I'd ever done. Even now, hours later, I was practically overwhelmed by it all.

So overwhelmed I barely even registered the knock at my door until it started to grow more insistent. I sat up in bed, my heart in my throat. Ivy or Noelle would have just walked in. In fact, none of my friends ever knocked. I got up and tiptoed over to the door, trying to squelch my fear. It was 3 a.m. Why was someone at my dorm room door at 3 a.m.?

I held my breath, cracked the door, and got my answer. Josh Hollis's green eyes stared back at me, startled. I guess he was surprised I had finally answered.

"Oh my God," I whispered. I grabbed the arm of his wool coat and yanked him inside. "What the hell are you doing?"

"I'm sorry. I just . . . I had to—"

He looked at me for a long moment, as if he'd never seen me before. His bottom lip was cut and swollen, and there was a grayish-purple bruise around his left eye. I was about to break the awkward silence by asking if it hurt, when he suddenly reached for my arm and pulled me into him, wrapping his arms around me, practically swallowing me into his thick coat. I was so surprised I couldn't even think. This was all I'd wanted to do since we'd arrived back at Easton. This. This and nothing else. He held me so tight I could feel the muscles of his chest through his sweater. I closed my eyes and breathed him in. He smelled of dust and sweat and paint and fabric softener and fresh air. He smelled like Josh. Slightly dirty Josh, but Josh.

Then I realized what was happening, where we were, who was right next door, and I pulled away. Josh's face was almost desperate as I backed into my desk chair and gripped the top of it behind me for dear life. Suddenly I was acutely aware of my skimpy tank top and pajama shorts. Not exactly the appropriate attire for a middle-of-the-night encounter with the boyfriend of one of your good friends.

"How did you get in here?" I asked.

"I have a passkey," he said, looking away. "We got it last—"

He stopped. My grip on the chair back tightened. We both knew who the other half of "we" was, and I, for one, didn't want to think about her just now.

"Where have you been all day?" I whispered.

Josh shed his coat, dropping it on the floor near the door. He pushed his hands into his hair as he sat down on my bed. It let out a loud squeak and I instinctively looked at the wall, as if I could somehow see through it, to where Ivy was asleep right on the other side.

"I slept in the infirmary last night and Hathaway woke me up at five this morning to start my all-day detention," Josh explained.

"What?"

"Yeah." He looked up at me, clearly annoyed. "One full day, alone with Graham, cleaning out the basement rooms in Hell Hall."

I gulped. They had spent the day working in the basement at Hell? Why? Did the headmaster somehow know what had been going on down there, or was it just a coincidence? Had he found some stray matches I had missed? Had we left something else behind?

"He didn't let us go until midnight," Josh explained. "I was exhausted, but when I got back to my room I couldn't sleep."

He dropped back on the bed crossways so that his feet were still on the floor, and stared up at the ceiling. I took a breath and tried to remind myself that this was not about me or the BLS or our secret meetings. This was about Josh. The love of my life. Who, for some reason, was hanging out in my room instead of his girlfriend's.

"You were trapped in a room with Graham all day?" I asked, tentatively sitting down next to him.

"Yeah. That was fun," he said sarcastically. "Silence, all day. Neither of us said a word."

"Josh, what is it between the two of you?" I asked. "What happened at St. James Prep?"

Josh blew out a sigh and sat up. He rubbed the heel of his hand into his unbruised eye. "I don't want to talk about it. Not now."

I felt a twinge of irritation. But my frustration was quickly squelched by my sympathy for Josh. Just last night he'd gotten his ass kicked and then he'd spent nineteen hours doing manual labor. Was that kind of punishment even legal?

"I have to ask you something," he said.

"What?" I asked.

I wanted to touch his face. Tuck that stray curl back from his eye. Put my arm on his shoulder. Take his hand. Something. Anything. But I couldn't touch him. I wasn't allowed.

Josh tucked his chin slightly and pressed his hands together between his knees. "Are you and Sawyer . . . ?"

The world screeched to a halt. My throat constricted.

"Are Sawyer and I what?"

Josh got up and the bed squealed in protest again. He put his hands over his face and groaned in frustration, way too loudly for my comfort.

"I can't," he whispered vehemently. "I can't do this anymore, Reed. I don't . . . I don't love her. Not like I love you. It'll never be like it is with us. It doesn't matter what I do or . . . or how hard I try. She'll never be . . . She's not you."

I stared up at him, my breath coming short and ragged. Hot tears filled my eyes as my heart exploded over and over again, releasing all the hope and longing it had been holding inside for so long.

"So please," Josh said. "Please just tell me that you and Sawyer aren't . . . that you're not . . ."

He couldn't even finish the sentence. I stood up. My room was so small that the very act put us within inches of each other. I took one step and our foreheads touched. His fingertips grazed my waist and my entire body trembled. Then Josh slipped one hand around the small of my back, the other over my cheek. My hands fluttered to his chest. I looked into his eyes.

"I love you, Reed," he said.

I sighed three months' worth of sighs. "I love you too."

And then, shoving thoughts of Ivy and Sawyer and everything else in the world to the back of our minds, we finally, finally kissed.

FALLOUT

The next morning, the guilt had settled hard and heavy in the pit of my gut. By the light of day, when I wasn't wrapped up in the insane romance of the moment, I was nothing but a cheater and a backstabber. It didn't matter that I'd loved Josh first. It didn't matter that we wanted to be together. We could have waited until he'd broken up with her. We could have tried to explain. But now it was too late. We'd kissed. A lot. With Ivy right next door.

I loathed myself.

Then, the moment I walked into the dining hall on Monday morning, Constance scurried up to me all bright smiles and long red braids, and I started to wonder if I hadn't been better off stranded on that deserted island off St. Barths.

"Hey!" she said. "Listen, I know I'm not supposed to talk about it in public, but I thought, you know, we'd get our taps over the weekend. Are they coming today?"

The good news was the sisters of the BLS could keep a secret. The bad news was, I hadn't thought about all the things that were probably going to change as of this very moment. I glanced past her at Lorna, her roommate whom she'd been walking with before running ahead to greet me. How were these two going to live together once Constance knew that Lorna was in and she was out? Lorna hovered in the aisle next to the two Billings tables for a moment. At the first, Noelle, Portia, Tiffany, Kiki, Astrid, and Amberly were chatting away. The second was occupied by London, Vienna, and Missy. Lorna decided to join them and as she sat, I realized that she and Vienna looked miserable and uncomfortable, while the other two were oblivious. What were they going to do when they learned the truth?

The solid rock of guilt in my gut doubled in size. There was no point in dragging this out. Constance deserved to know what was going on. They all did.

"Actually, Constance," I said, keeping my voice low as a gaggle of freshmen gabbed their way by, "initiation already happened . . . last night."

It took way too long for the meaning of this to dawn on Constance's face. When it did, her eyes widened for a brief moment, as if she'd just heard a gunshot, and then everything crumbled.

"What!?" she shrieked.

The entire population of Easton turned around to stare. Gritting my teeth, I tugged her toward the back wall.

"Constance," I said quietly. "I'm sorry, okay? I know you're upset, but three people had to be cut, and you had the lowest score on knowledge night and didn't even show up for work night."

"I told you! I had to talk to Whit that night! He needed me," Constance cried.

"I know, but the book says—"

Tears spilled over onto Constance's freckled cheek. "I don't give a shit what the book says!" she blurted. Then her hand flew up to cover her mouth. Constance never cursed. Ever.

"How could you leave me out, Reed?" Constance whispered, her bottom lip trembling. "You're my best friend."

Okay, I was scum. Slutty, cheating, backstabbing scum. In that moment, none of it mattered. Not the book or the alumna who'd given it to me. Not the history or the legacy or the tradition. All that mattered was I'd broken my friend's heart.

"Constance—"

I reached for her arm, but she yanked it away. "I can't believe you'd do this to me, Reed. I'm the only one who's always been your friend no matter what," she whispered, her eyes so fierce I was startled. "When you ditched us last year to go live in Billings, I was still there. When everyone else voted to kick you out, I was one of *three people* who took your side. But you . . . you don't care about me at all, do you? All you care about is your elitist Billings Girls. Well, guess what? I wouldn't even join your stupid secret society if you paid me!"

My lungs felt as if they were full of mucky water. I couldn't breathe through all the guilt. She turned around and ran for the table, where she leaned over and whispered in Missy's ear before grabbing her stuff and storming out.

Missy whirled around, her thick French braid flying, and leveled me with a glare that could have taken out the entire US Army. As she got up, I saw London starting to realize something was amiss. Vienna pulled her aside to explain. This was a disaster.

"Well, thanks, Reed," Missy said, crossing her arms as she stood in front of me. "You've finally proved what I've always known about you—you *are* a liar."

"Excuse me?" I said, shocked.

"Weren't you the one who was always talking about including everyone? Opening up Billings to different classes, different backgrounds, different everything?" Missy whispered, narrowing her eyes. "Then the second you get the slightest bit of power, you're ostracizing the people you claim are your friends."

"It's not my fault," I said. "There could only be eleven—"

"Oh, please!" Missy said with a sneer. "What did you think was going to happen if you let all of us in? Do you think Elizabeth Williams and Theresa Billings are going to rise from their graves and stalk you down? Give me a break. You're just pissed about what happened last semester and you're trying to put all of us in our places, show everyone who's in charge. Well, good for you, Reed."

We both glanced behind her as London burst into tears and headed for the bathroom, Vienna at her heels.

Missy raised her palms and let them slap down at her sides. "You walk around this school like you're so perfect, like you're everyone's friend, but you just proved one thing: You have *no* idea what it means to be a friend."

Then Missy turned on her heel and walked out through the same door through which Constance had exited moments ago. I stood there for a long moment, my stomach quivering, and tried to catch my breath. The nine girls left at the Billings tables watched me with a mixture of sympathy and concern. I was about to push myself away from the wall when Josh emerged from the food line, a pile of dough-nuts on his tray. He was a good thirty yards away, but directly across from me, and we both stopped in our tracks. My body reacted to the sight of him in a way that was totally incongruous with my current state of shame.

Then Ivy came through the far door and spotted him instantly. She rushed over and planted a huge kiss right on Josh's lips.

"I thought you were dead!" she scolded him, giving him a whack on the shoulder before dragging him over to their usual table.

Right. That was it. No breakfast for me. I hightailed it out of there as fast as I could, one awful thought repeating itself over and over in my mind.

Missy, of all people, was right. I was a liar. A hypocrite. And I had no idea what it meant to be a friend.

THE CREED

That night, as my new sisters and I settled in among the piles of pillows and blankets we'd squirreled up to the old chapel for our first official meeting, I tried to put all the negative thoughts and emotions of the last eighteen hours out of my mind. All day I'd been enduring betrayed glares from Constance, Missy, and London, the three of whom were suddenly inseparable. Everywhere I went, there they were in a tight knot—during morning services, at lunch, in the library. At dinner, they'd sat at a separate table and Shelby had actually joined them, making the circle of Reed-haters complete. By the time I tossed out my uneaten meal, I was wondering what the hell I'd been thinking, agreeing to keep the BLS down to eleven members. Would four more members really have been such a big deal? Who was to say that Elizabeth Williams hadn't picked the number eleven simply because the love of her life was born in November? Or because she had eleven pairs of shoes? It could have been a totally arbitrary thing, and now I'd made myself and four of my friends miserable over it.

It was too late to change it. Even if I somehow convinced Ivy we were wrong, I didn't think any of the four ousted Billings Girls were going to want to join us now. And as if all of the Billings insanity wasn't bad enough, all day I'd also avoided Sawyer as much as possible, afraid he might try to hold my hand or solidify a date or, worst of all, kiss me again. And then there was Ivy. I hadn't talked to her once today, certain that if I tried, I wouldn't be able to look her in the eye.

But now there she was, lowering herself onto a huge purple pillow directly across the circle from me. Had she spoken to Josh? Had he said anything to her about last night? I had to believe he hadn't, or she'd currently be either pulling my hair out or not here at all. But if he hadn't said anything to her, what did that mean? Was he going to stay with her, still? He had for this long. Why should I believe that last night had changed anything?

"Reed? Could you scooch over? I need some leg room."

I blinked up at Tiffany as she tried to settle in next to me with her cushion and blanket.

"Oh. Sure." I slid my own pillow aside to give her more room, internally vowing to put all thoughts of Josh and Ivy out of my mind. For now.

We'd pushed aside the moveable benches in the choir area behind the pulpit and surrounded the space with candles. It was far more cozy and sisterly than arranging ourselves in the pews. The book was open on the floor in front of me so I could reference it if I needed to during the course of the meeting. Everyone else had brought snacks and drinks, but all of it was tucked away for now, until the opening ritual was completed.

Noelle was the last to arrive. She let the door of the chapel slam as she walked in.

"Should we really be meeting here again?" she said loudly, her voice bouncing off the high ceiling. "Double H isn't stupid. If we keep coming to the same place every other night, he's going to figure it out."

"Shhhh!" I scolded her. "We haven't started the meeting yet."

Noelle dropped her black Kate Spade bag on the floor and whipped off her jacket. "Sorry," she said sarcastically. She dropped a puffy pillow on the floor between Amberly and Tiffany and sat down, crossing her legs at the ankle in the center of the circle. "So, all-fabulous BLS guru, what do we do first? Because I, for one, am starved." She turned and rustled around in her bag, coming out with a box of gourmet chocolates, a sleeve of crackers, and a wedge of wrapped cheese. "Shall we?"

A few of the girls clapped and reached for the food. I gritted my teeth.

"I have to officially open the meeting first," I said.

Noelle crunched into a cracker. "Why? Does it say anything in there about not speaking with your mouth full?" she asked, nodding at the book.

I rolled my eyes. "No. It doesn't, but—"

"How about not getting caught?" Noelle asked. "Because, seriously, we're like sitting ducks up here and I—"

"Noelle," I said loudly.

Everyone froze. Astrid withdrew her hand, which had been reaching across the circle for the cheese, back behind her.

Noelle raised her eyebrows at me. She licked a bit of cracker from her bottom lip and waited. "Yes?" she said finally.

"This chapel is where the original Billings Literary Society met, and it is where we will meet until *I* decide it's unsafe and initiate a vote on the matter," I said succinctly. "Now, as for the food, I would appreciate it if you'd have some respect for the society's rituals and put it aside until I've called the meeting to order."

My heart pounded with nerves. Putting Noelle in her place was not an easy thing to do. What if she just got up and walked out? Would the others follow? Although I supposed that would be a good way to figure out whether anyone truly saw me as an authority figure around here.

Noelle took a breath and made a big show of gathering up her food and piling it up behind her.

"Better?" she asked.

My heart breathed a sigh of relief.

"Much," I replied.

I turned and handed out the handwritten copies I'd made of the Billings Literary Society's creed.

"We will recite this at the beginning of each meeting," I said. "This first time, you can read from the page, but we'll spend some of our time here tonight memorizing it so we can burn these copies. I don't want there to be any chance that these will be found."

A few of the girls nodded. Kiki was already reciting the creed under her breath, committing the words to memory.

"All right then. Let's begin."

Together, we read the creed aloud.

"We, the sisters of the Billings Literary Society, do hereby pledge our hearts and minds to the purposes of the Society."

As our voices melded together in the night, a chill went through me. This was it. This was what I'd been working toward for the past two weeks. I'd brought the Billings Literary Society back from the forgotten annals of history.

"We promise to be loyal, steadfast, and true to all who join our circle. We vow never to reveal the secrets of our society, but to uphold its values and standards in the face of all tyranny."

Pride prickled my skin as I looked around at each of my friends, having long since memorized the words myself. Tiffany and Rose gazed back at me with content smiles. Kiki, Astrid, and even Amberly had never looked so stoic and alert. They felt it, too, the import of what we were doing here. I could tell.

"Blood to blood, ashes to ashes, sister to sister, we make this sacred vow."

I looked at Noelle as we finished the creed, wanting more than anything for her to feel it too—to know she understood why I was doing this, why it mattered. She smiled, reached behind her, and grabbed her crackers.

"All right," she said. "Let's get this party started."

Everyone whooped and hollered and dove into their own stashes of goodies. Kiki chucked a Hostess cupcake at me and I caught it with both hands, letting out a laugh. I decided right then and there to let the seriousness go for now. We'd all worked hard to get here. It was about time we had a little fun.

THE SISTERHOOD

"Reed! This secret-society thing was the best idea ever!" Portia said, throwing her arm around me as we gathered our things at the end of the night.

I laughed and hugged her back. "I'm glad you think so."

It turned out that Vienna had brought champagne, which had livened things up considerably. I'd managed to get them to spend fifteen minutes memorizing the creed, another five burning the pages over a candle near the window, and ten more discussing issues of the day, just like the original sisters of the BLS did almost a century ago. And then, everything had deteriorated into a full-out party.

But instead of scolding them or trying to get their attention, I'd decided to go with the "If you can't beat 'em, join 'em," approach. Part of the point of being together was to have fun, and after all the work I'd done to get the BLS up and running, and all the misery of the day, I felt like I deserved a little fun.

"So, Kiki, you're going to design a new insignia, right?" I said, folding my red throw over my arm. We had decided, via unanimous vote, that the BLS crest needed a twenty-first-century update and Kiki, aspiring graphic artist that she was, had offered to work on it.

"I'm on it like white on rice," she said with a nod and a salute. "I'll have some ideas by the next meeting."

"And they're going to be awesome!" Amberly trilled, dancing in a circle in the center of the floor. The lightweight had downed way too much bubbly for her own good.

Astrid, who had figured out the tune of the secret whistle, was standing in the aisle trying to teach it to Rose and Tiffany, while Vienna, Lorna, and Noelle lay in the center of the floor, trying to figure out what the image in the broken stained-glass window behind the pulpit had once been.

"Come on, frosh," Ivy said, nudging Amberly with her hip. "I'll walk you back to your dorm."

"You will!? Oh, *cool*, Sister Ivy!" Amberly trilled, throwing her arms around Ivy's neck.

"You barf on me, you die," Ivy said, wrinkling her nose at me.

I glanced away the second her eyes met mine, bending to the floor to grab the book and my messenger bag.

"Reed? Is everything okay?" Ivy asked.

I stood up, bit my lip quickly, then turned to face her. "Yeah! Why?" I said, far too brightly.

"You just seem . . . different," she said, narrowing her eyes.

"I think I'm just tired," I replied, moving toward the door. "I've been really busy with all the planning and stuff. I think I just need some rest."

Rest I should have been getting last night when I was smooching your boyfriend in the wee hours of the morning.

My throat constricted and I looked away. My eyes fell on a woven leather band Ivy wore on one wrist. Dangling from it was a small silver medallion with a red and yellow design on it. Instantly I thought of Tattoo Guy and his red and yellow neck tattoo and I felt a rush of possibility. Maybe he and Ivy *did* have something going. Maybe they *were* flirting that morning. Which meant that maybe, just maybe, she wouldn't be so entirely crushed about what had happened between me and Josh. Maybe she was ready to move on, too, and just hadn't said it yet.

Suddenly I felt a whole lot lighter.

"Well, don't worry," she said, holding on to Amberly with one hand and putting her other arm around me for a squeeze. "Look around. You did it. The BLS is back. You should relax and just enjoy it."

I shrugged away from her, lifting my bag over my head as an excuse. "Yeah. You're right. No more stress allowed."

We all walked out through the front door together, talking and laughing. Tiffany and I tried to shush the other girls, but our efforts were met with a round of laughter. Once we got outside I was really going to have to try to convince them to shut the heck up before we got back to campus, or this thing was going to be over before it got started. I held the door open for the group, then turned around and found all of my friends standing in a clump, being stared down by a wall of women.

My feet slipped in the snow and Ivy grabbed me to keep me from going down. My friends went mute. A second glance told me it wasn't so much of a wall as it was a group of three people, two of whom I recognized. Suzel and Paige Ryan—the girl whose mother had tried to murder me over the course of a few weeks in St. Barths. The third woman was older, perhaps in her midfifties, with jet-black curls and lines around her light blue eyes. They were all wearing black coats and black hats, Paige's a fedora, Suzel's a wide-brim, the third woman's laced with fur.

"Paige! Suzel! Demetria!" Noelle said, stepping forward in the crowd. "What are you all doing here?"

"Noelle," Suzel said coolly, looking Noelle up and down with a flick of her gaze. "I hardly expected to find *you* here."

Noelle glanced behind her at the rest of us. I realized all at once that she had, as usual, automatically assumed the role of point person. I stepped up next to her, even though closing the distance between myself and Paige Ryan made my skin crawl.

"How did you find us?" I asked, glancing sideways at Noelle, who was probably gloating over being right. Well, almost right. We'd been snagged at our meeting place, just not by Headmaster Hathaway.

"We came here tonight to give you girls fair warning," the third woman, Demetria, said, ignoring my question. "The Billings alumni committee is willing to ignore this little project of yours, whatever it is," she said, looking at the chapel with distaste. "As long as you cease and desist now."

"What do we care whether you ignore it or not?" I asked, giving her a dubious look.

"Reed," Noelle warned through her teeth.

"I told you," Suzel said to Demetria.

"Oh, you care," Paige spoke up. The wind tossed a few of her auburn curls in front of her face and she shoved them away with her gloved hand. "If you don't give up, we'll be forced to report you, or worse."

"Don't even talk to me," I spat, looking her up and down with ire. "As far as I'm concerned, you *and* your crazy family can kiss my ass."

A couple of my friends laughed. Demetria's lips pursed sourly. I stepped toward her, lifting my chin.

"I don't know who you are, but I'm here to tell you that your day is done," I said firmly. "All of you. This is our time, and we may no longer have a house to keep us together, but we have each other. As for the Billings alumni committee, I think it's about time you ladies got over your glory days and moved on."

Demetria made an offended noise in the back of her throat, but I didn't care. She might have been a Billings alumna, but clearly she was not aware of the book. Clearly she, like Suzel, had never even heard of the Billings Literary Society. Which meant she was nothing to me. I turned my back on her and the others and trudged off through the snow, my friends forming a snaking line behind me.

"Nice work, Reed!" Ivy said, catching up with me. "That was awesome!"

"It so was not," Noelle countered, walking on my other side. "You can't just tell those women off, Reed. We need them."

"For what?" I said, stopping in my tracks. The rest of the girls gathered around me. I was starting to feel like a magnet with a parade of metal shards following my every move. "In case you haven't noticed, Billings House no longer exists."

"Maybe not, but the alumni pay for everything. Parties, trips, supplies. They're the ones who kept you in designer labels all last semester, in case you've forgotten," Noelle said, crossing her arms over her chest.

"I haven't forgotten," I replied. "But that's not what Billings is about anymore, Noelle." I lifted my hands toward the group of girls behind me. "It's about us. The sisterhood. I no longer need any of the stuff those women can give me. All I need is my friends."

With that I turned my back on a stunned Noelle and flounced down the hill, every single one of my sisters at my back.

THE TRUTH

Hypocrite. Hypocrite, hypocrite, hypocrite.

I heard the word in my mind over and over again with every move I made.

Climbing the stairs in Pemberly with Ivy, Noelle and Lorna: *HYP-o-crite! HYP-o-crite!*

Brushing my teeth up and down: *Hyp-o-CRITE! Hyp-o-CRITE!*

Cranking my window open to let the cold chase out the heat: *Hypocritehypcocritehypocrite!*

Finally, I couldn't take it anymore. I had stood there in the woods and preached to Noelle about how all I needed was my friends, my sisters, but I was lying to one of them. Lying about the worst thing imaginable. I couldn't do it anymore. If I was going to be a true leader of the Billings Literary Society, if I was going to call myself a real friend, I had to be honest. Whatever the fallout, I would just have to deal with it.

Please just let me be right about Ivy and Tattoo Guy. It would make all of this so much easier.

I shoved myself out of bed and knocked lightly on Ivy's door. She answered immediately. We had only just left each other in the bathroom five minutes ago. Behind her, Jillian snored lightly in her bed. Ivy slipped out into the hall in her gray cotton nightshirt and closed the door with a quiet click.

"What's up?" she asked, leaning sideways against the cream-colored wall. "Are you freaking about what happened up at the chapel?"

"No," I said, my heart throbbing in my throat. "It's not about that. There's . . . there's something I need to tell you. You're going to hate me, but I have to tell you."

Ivy's face fell. She stood up straight. "What?" she asked flatly.

Suddenly I couldn't imagine how I was supposed to put this. All the words in the English language were jammed up in my throat, held back by my painfully expanding heart.

"Reed, you're freaking me out here," Ivy said, backing up a step. "What is it?"

I swallowed as hard as I could. Every inch of my skin burned with dread at what I was about to do. But she deserved to know. Josh and I were in love. He'd said it himself. Nothing he did could change it. Ivy deserved better than a boyfriend who didn't love her and a best friend who was lying to her.

"Josh and I kissed," I blurted.

Ivy's jaw dropped and she bent at the waist slightly, hugging her slim arms around her. "What? When?"

"Last night," I said miserably, looking at the floor. "I'm sorry. I didn't plan it or anything. It just kind of—"

"Where? I didn't even see him until this morning," Ivy said, her face contorted with confusion and anger.

I bit the inside of my cheek. This was not going to go over well. "Here. In my room. He came . . . here."

Ivy looked at my door, her lip curling in disgust. "Omigod," she said, her hand fluttering up to cover her mouth. When she turned to me again, her eyes were brimming with tears. "You are such a fucking bitch!"

Her words filled the hallway. A couple of lights flicked on, their glow illuminating the cracks between the doors and the floor.

"Ivy—"

"No. No. Don't even talk to me!" Ivy shouted, opening the door of her room. "I thought we were friends. All that crap about how much *you* trust *me* and now you're sneaking around behind my back!? What's the matter with you?"

Jillian came to the door, blinking herself awake. "What's going on? Are you okay?" she asked Ivy.

"Yeah, I'm fine," Ivy said, stepping inside. She looked me in the eye with abhorrence. "I just should've known better than to trust a Billings Girl."

Then she slammed the door so hard one of the paintings on the hallway wall crashed to the ground. She might as well have just sliced through my gut with a kitchen knife. As I turned around, several open doors quickly closed, none of my dorm mates wanting to get caught spying. I slipped back inside my room, trembling from head to toe, and sat down on my bed.

I had thought that telling the truth was supposed to be the right thing. And Ivy had to know, didn't she? Better she find out from me than walk in on me and Josh kissing or something. But as I heard Ivy crying to Jillian next door, I had a feeling Ivy would have preferred not to have known. And I felt worse than ever.

THE REJECT TABLE

"This is going to be a problem," Noelle said as she lowered herself into the chair next to mine at breakfast. "Check the reject table."

For the first time in fifteen minutes I lifted my gaze from my slowly eroding Cheerios. I'd been the first student to walk into the dining hall that morning, and hadn't even noticed that other people were starting to arrive. Noelle, the first person to join me at our table, was looking across the aisle at Constance, Missy, London, and Shelby. The four of them had been sitting together at every meal since the previous morning, but today, there were some new faces among the crowd. Amberly's roommate, Cassie Something-or-Other and Ivy's roommate, Jillian, who looked like a snarling lion the second she saw me watching. Clearly she hated me for what had happened with Ivy in the middle of the night.

Honestly, I was kind of surprised Ivy wasn't over there too. From under the brim of my baseball cap—which was hiding my unwashed hair—I scanned the rest of the room. No sign of Ivy or Josh. Where were they? Off together somewhere fighting? Or worse . . . making up?

"I don't know. It makes sense," I said, pushing my juice glass around in the circle of condensation beneath it. "Of course they're all going to hang out together."

"Yeah, but now they have followers," Noelle said, spreading some butter onto her bagel while keeping an eye on the rejects. "And also, they know where we meet."

I saw Kiki, Astrid, and Vienna enter the food line. London spotted them too and said something obviously mocking that made everyone at her table crack up laughing. Was it possible that the BLS had actually managed to come between the Twin Cities? That seemed like a crime against nature. I'd never told anyone that we couldn't be friends with the people who didn't make the cut. And London and Vienna were the closest friends I'd ever known. The idea that I'd been instrumental in splitting them up was beyond depressing.

Maybe this whole thing was a mistake. Maybe I should just disband the BLS and let everyone get on with their lives. Just like Noelle had said that first morning back. But when I looked at her across the table, I bristled at the very thought of telling her she'd been right all along.

"How do you figure that?" I asked, taking a tentative bite of my cereal. My stomach clenched and I put the spoon down.

"Come on, Reed," Noelle said, rolling her eyes. "You took them all up to the chapel. They're not stupid. One of them has to have figured out that we were cleaning that place up for a reason."

I glanced over at the table again. I couldn't imagine Constance or London putting two and-two together on that score, and Shelby was far too involved with her own little world to think much about why she'd spent a couple of hours doing nothing in a chapel in the woods. But Missy . . . Missy definitely might have figured it out.

"I bet one of them told the Billings alumni and that's how they found us there last night," Noelle said.

"What? Come on. They wouldn't report us, would they? They all know Hathaway would expel us," I said. "They can't hate us enough to get us thrown out of school."

"They didn't tell Hathaway. They told Billings," Noelle said, taking a bite of her bagel. "I can just imagine Missy calling up Paige and whining all over her."

"Wait. Missy knows Paige?" I asked.

Noelle looked at me like I'd just taken out a razor and shaved half my hair off. "They're cousins. Like second or third or once removed or something, but still."

"What?" I blurted. "I never knew that."

"Oh, come on. Someone must've mentioned it at some point."

This was insane. Missy was the biggest show-off at Easton, and Paige was, like, Billings royalty. My mind reeled, but it almost felt good. It was nice to be focusing on something other than how horrible I was.

Across the room, a skinny freshman dropped his tray and the entire room applauded at the clatter.

"I wouldn't put it past Missy," I said finally. "She's hated me since before I was ever in Billings."

"Yeah, and her family would *not* be pleased about the BLS," Noelle said, sipping her coffee.

"What do you mean?" I asked. Amberly, Lorna, and Rose had joined the other BLS sisters on the food line, which was starting to swell as the people who got up at a normal hour trickled in.

Noelle glanced at me, swallowed, and touched her napkin to her lips. "Nothing. They're just . . . all about propriety. They wouldn't like the idea that we've turned the revered Billings House into a group of girls hiding out in the woods."

I watched her carefully, feeling as if there was something more. Something else about Missy that she wasn't saying.

"Anyway, now that we've been outed, we definitely need to find a new meeting space, and I have a couple of ideas," Noelle said. As she started going on about the Art Cemetery and a little-known private study area of the library, I felt this eerie sense of déjà vu. It felt exactly like the time I'd been trying to plan a party in the city for a Billings fund-raiser and Noelle had swooped in to change the venue at the last minute. She was trying to take charge again. Trying to elbow me out. And I wasn't going to let it happen.

Even if I did, on some level, agree with her.

"No," I said, cutting her off midsentence.

"No?" she replied, flummoxed.

"The chapel is where the original BLS met, and that's where we're going to stay," I told her.

Noelle looked at me for a moment, incredulous, then dropped her bagel and smacked her hands together, as if she was wiping her hands of me.

"Fine. If that's the way you want it, then fine," she said.

"So, what? Are you going to quit now?" I asked.

Noelle sighed and looked at me, her wrists resting on the edge of the table. "No, my dear fearless leader. I will follow you into the pits of hell if that's what you want me to do," she said with a facetious smile. "Just like all your other little minions."

I wasn't sure, exactly, what her sarcasm was supposed to be getting at, but I decided to just take her words at face value.

"Good," I said, taking a bite of my toast. "That's what I like to hear."

As the other BLS sisters started to settle in around us, I kept one eye on the reject table and one eye on the door, waiting for Josh or Ivy to arrive. What did it mean that the first enemy I'd made at Easton—Missy Thurber—was related to the woman who had tried to murder me—Clarissa Ryan? Or was it just a coincidence?

Only one thing was certain: If Missy was working against me and the BLS, I was going to find out.

RECORD PACE

Ever since returning from St. Barths, I'd been trying not to think about it. Trying not to relive that night. But somehow my conversation with Noelle at breakfast had sparked the memories and now I couldn't keep them at bay. As I sat in Spanish class, waiting for Mr. Shreeber to arrive, I kept seeing Mrs. Ryan's dressing room. The perfume bottle on her nightstand. The sweatshirt hanging in her closet—the one she'd worn when she pushed me off her boat on the night after Christmas. Mrs. Ryan returning to the room with that tray full of food. How her smile had turned wild and sinister as soon as she realized I knew.

When she'd attacked me, I'd been too weak to really fight back. Too dehydrated and starved and spent. I'd thought I was truly going to die. That the fifth time she tried to kill me was going to be the charm.

But then Sawyer had rushed into the room and saved me. Without even the merest thought for himself, he'd saved my life. For a second time.

"Reed."

I turned around, startled, to find Sawyer standing there in the flesh. One hand clutched the strap of his navy blue backpack. The other, the one with the woven bracelets around the wrist, pressed into my desk.

"Hey, Sawyer!" I said with a smile, even as my nerves sizzled at the memory of our kiss and his expectations of relationship. "What's up?"

"I heard about you and Josh," he said. "Is it true?"

I was so stunned I couldn't speak. I just stared at him blankly, my mouth yawning open like a cave.

"I heard you guys hooked up on Sunday night," Sawyer said, keeping his voice low. "Is it true?" he repeated.

"Sawyer—"

"It is." He looked down at his feet and his face grew mottled with red. "I'm such an idiot."

"No. You're not," I said, feeling that now familiar guilt rise up in my chest. "I am. I'm the idiot."

The chairs around us were starting to fill up. I caught a few curious glances and sighed. I'd been at the center of more than a few scenes in the last couple of days and I didn't like it.

"Who told you? Ivy?" I asked.

He shook his head. "Graham."

I blinked, surprised. "How did *Graham* know?"

"Does it matter?" He paused and placed his hand in his pocket, then seemed to gather his courage before he looked up at me. "I thought that you . . . I mean, I thought that we . . ."

I gulped back my guilt and misery as Mr. Shreeber walked into the room. "I'm sorry, Sawyer. But . . . we're friends. I think that's all we're going to be."

Sawyer's mouth flattened in to a grim line.

"We *are* friends, right?" I asked tentatively.

"Good morning, class! Let's take our seats," Mr. Shreeber called out, clapping his hands together once. "We have a lot to cover today!"

With that, Sawyer turned around and walked to his desk in the back of the room. For the rest of the class period, he didn't look away from the board once, and when the bell rang, he was out of there faster than you can say "heartbreaker."

I stood up from my chair shakily, feeling dejected and suddenly exhausted. I was losing friends at a record pace, even for me. All thanks to the BLS and Josh. As I made my way out of the room to the continued curious glances of my classmates, all I could do was hope that both would prove to be worth it.

KISS A WUSS

That evening, studying alone in my room, I decided to call another meeting of the Billings Literary Society for Wednesday night. Between Noelle's sarcasm, my fight with Ivy, the growing crowd at the anti-Billings table, and our encounter with the Billings alumnae, my brand-new secret society was already on seriously shaky ground. I needed to know that everyone was still with me. That Noelle wasn't going to bail. That the others weren't going to get skittish.

And I wanted to talk to Ivy. All day I'd only seen her from afar. She always seemed to be in a rush to get wherever she was going, her cell phone, permanently attached to her ear. Even though I was sending her telepathic messages to talk to me, to look at me, to feel me watching her, she never glanced at me once. It was as if I'd become invisible.

It wasn't that I didn't understand. I had done something awful. Something that was maybe even unforgivable. But at least I'd owned up to it. I'd never done that with Noelle after my five minutes of debauchery with Dash. Although that had been slightly different, since technically they were broken up at the time and technically we'd both been drugged. Josh and I had known exactly what we were doing, and he and Ivy were definitely together when we were doing it.

Yeah. She was never going to forgive me.

Still, her name was on the e-mail that went out to all the sisters of the BLS, asking them to meet at the chapel at 11 p.m. on Wednesday night. I had to know if she would come. If the society mattered more to her than my stupid actions did.

The moment I clicked "send" there was a knock on my door. I jumped to answer it. Josh slipped inside, his hair glistening with snow. My heart instantly slammed into overdrive. He looked . . . excited. It was amazing how his very presence made me forget all about my guilt, my regret, my hope for winning Ivy back.

"You have to stop coming here after hours. You're going to get me in trouble," I said with a grin, not meaning a word.

"Ivy and I broke up," he whispered.

"Really? Oh." I took a breath, trying to edit the four thousand questions and comments fighting for the tip of my tongue. I glanced in the direction of her room.

"She's not here," he said, reading my thoughts. "She's at the solarium."

"Okay." I crossed my arms over my stomach, trying not to think of how Ivy must have felt at that moment. "I guess you know I told her."

"Yeah. She wasn't happy." He slipped his coat off and dropped it on the back of my chair. I suddenly realized the "sent" list was still up from my BLS e-mail and I casually closed my laptop. As much as I loved Josh and wanted to share everything with him, the Billings Literary Society was going to remain a secret, even from him.

"I'm sorry," I said, kneading my palm between my thumb and forefinger. "But if I were in her position, I would have wanted to know."

"I get it," Josh said, running his hands through his hair. He sat down on my bed and looked up through his curls. "Honestly, I was kind of glad I didn't have to break it to her. I mean, I would have. I know I should have, but . . ." He hung his head. "Does that make me a wuss?" he asked sheepishly.

"Kind of, yeah," I joked.

Josh reached up, grabbed my wrist, and pulled me onto his lap. My heart swooped over and over like a paper airplane tumbling through the sky.

"Care to kiss a wuss?" he asked.

"Eh, why not?" I replied.

And then he kissed me. And kissed me and kissed me and kissed me until I forgot where we were, forgot to wonder what it might mean, forgot about who we might hurt.

He kissed me until all that mattered was us.

THE HATHAWAY MEN

Josh was waiting for me outside Pemberly the next morning. The sky was a perfect bright blue and the air was still. I paused when I saw him there, looking freshly showered and adorable, his green wool turtleneck grazing his chin above the collar of his coat. He reached for my hand. I took it. Nothing had ever felt so amazing as his warm, rough fingers closing around mine.

"So, we're doing this?" I said, my heart pounding erratically.

"We're doing this," he replied firmly.

I grinned. "All right then."

We turned up the path toward the dining hall and I had to concentrate to keep from skipping. No one in the world was happier than me at that moment. I wished I could float in the feeling for days. Josh squeezed my hand and smiled and I knew he felt the same. This was the way it was supposed to be. Josh and Reed. Together.

Then Graham and Sawyer walked out the back door of Ketlar. The bottom of my stomach dropped out. They were about to turn toward the dining hall as well, but as soon as Sawyer saw us—saw my fingers entwined with Josh's—he turned on his heel and stormed off in the opposite direction, taking the path that ran along the dorms. Graham looked furious as he followed after his brother. I knew why Sawyer was mad, but for the ten millionth time, I had to wonder about Graham.

"Josh, can you please just tell me what happened between you and Graham Hathaway?" I asked. "Why does he get all clenched every time he sees you?"

We had come across one of the many stone benches that dotted the campus. Josh blew out a sigh and checked his watch. "Let's sit."

Whoa. I needed to sit down to hear this?

"Okay."

We sat on the cold bench. My butt froze instantly. I shifted and crossed my legs so only one cheek was resting fully on the frigid surface. Josh kept his grip on my hand and looked at his lap.

"The thing with Graham is . . . I used to go out with his twin sister, Jen," Josh said.

My throat closed over. Didn't I know someone else who had once dated Jen Hathaway? Oh yeah. Upton Giles. The *last* guy I'd kissed. I guess Sawyer had been right that morning at Shutters—Jen and I did have a lot in common. Including our taste in men.

"You know about Jen?" Josh asked, looking me in the eye. "You know how she . . ."

"Yeah," I said. "I didn't know she and Graham were twins, but . . . Sawyer told me how she died."

On the island. He'd told me about how his sister had committed suicide over the summer. How she hadn't left a note. How I reminded him of her. How we both should have steered clear of Upton.

Just like that my brain was off on a whole new tangent. Should I tell Josh about Upton? The two of us were still texting and e-mailing, but we were just friends now. Did it matter that a few weeks ago we were more than that?

"We were together for a few months my sophomore year," Josh was saying, toying with my fingers. "But things did not end well."

He let out a rueful scoff that begged a thousand questions, but my brain was too crowded to ask them.

"Anyway, Graham blamed me and I think that now that Jen's gone it's even harder for him," Josh continued. "I don't know if he's pissed at her or pissed at the world in general, but. . ."

"That sucks," I said finally, recrossing my legs so my right butt cheek could defrost. "I mean, I guess I get it, but it still sucks. I really like Graham. When he's not, you know, beating up on my man."

Josh let out a short laugh. "I do too," he said, staring off in the direction in which the Hathaway boys had disappeared. "Or I did. We used to be pretty good friends."

"How long had it been since you talked to Jen?" I asked. "I mean, did you ever talk before she—"

The sound of jaunty whistling distracted me and I stopped mid-sentence. Good thing, because coming down the path was Jen's father, Headmaster Hathaway, his hands in his pockets as he strolled along. When he saw me sitting there, he started to smile his headmastery smile, but then he saw who I was with and he just kept walking. Just like that. No "hello." No "good morning." No attempt at playing the BFF headmaster. Josh averted his eyes as Double H passed us by, and my stomach turned.

It was a clean sweep. I had officially lost all three Hathaway men as friends and allies. I looked at Josh and we both smiled tentatively. It was an awkward situation, no doubt—our headmaster being the father of the boys who hated us.

But at least we were in it together.

LET'S GET THIS PARTY STARTED

I waited outside the chapel on Wednesday night, freezing under my wool coat, my feet jittery inside my snow boots, though that was more from nerves than the cold. Kiki and Astrid were the first to arrive, followed by Amberly and Lorna. Tiffany and Rose emerged from the trees together, blankets folded over their arms. Portia and Vienna toted a bag full of clinking bottles. I was going to have to talk to them about this. We couldn't have champagne at every meeting or the Billings Girls were going to start flunking out of school.

Soon everyone was safely tucked inside except Noelle and Ivy. I glanced at my watch. Ten minutes past the meeting time. I took a breath and tipped my head back, watching the cloud of steam billow against the bare branches overhead. I would give them five more minutes. Then I was cutting my losses.

I heard a crunch and my head snapped down again. Noelle was walking purposefully toward me, carrying a white bakery box by its strings.

"I heard about what happened with Ivy," she said, lifting the box. "Figured a Fat Phoebe party was in order."

I smiled. It was the first moment since we'd returned from the islands that things felt absolutely normal between me and Noelle. Had I been wrong all along about the source of her attitude shift? Maybe it wasn't that some Billings alumna had chosen to share the book with me and not her. Maybe she was simply jealous of my friendship with Ivy. It made sense. Because now here we were, smiling and comfortable—now that it seemed my relationship with Ivy was kaput.

I wasn't exactly sure how I felt about that. I was glad Noelle was offering an olive branch, but why did it have to come at the expense of my friendship with Ivy? "Thanks," I said finally.

"So, I guess she's not coming, huh?" Noelle said, turning to look out at the trees.

"Doesn't look like it."

"I wouldn't count me out just yet."

The voice startled both of us so much that Noelle and I grabbed cach other's arms. Ivy emerged from the trees in a long black coat and black wool hat, her hands in her pockets. She hadn't brought a thing with her—not a bag, a pillow, or anything—and the lack of bulk made her seem even slimmer than usual. Her pale skin practically glowed against the black sky, her high cheekbones severe with her hair pulled back from her face

"Ivy! Hey," I said tentatively. My pulse raced with nervous anticipation as she paused in front of us. Was she here to hear me out or tear me to shreds? Her expression was so impassive it was impossible to tell.

"I'll be inside," Noelle said, slipping away without so much as a nod in Ivy's direction.

Ivy didn't seem to notice, however. Her gaze was fixed on me.

"Ivy, I'm so—"

She held up a black-gloved hand. "Don't. I feel bad enough as it is."

I almost fell over. "*You* feel bad?"

"I overreacted," Ivy said, taking a step closer. Her slick black boots slid under the upper layer of hard snow, her toes disappearing beneath the surface. "The truth is . . . things with Josh weren't right. I was trying too hard, you know? I should have broken up with him weeks ago, but I just . . . I didn't want to be alone. Not yet."

I swallowed hard. She didn't want to be alone after the shooting. That was the implied meaning. Again, it all came back to being my fault.

"And I guess I also didn't want to admit that he wasn't in love with me," she said. "He was still in love with you."

I looked down at my feet, my toes hovering off the edge of the crumbling redbrick steps. "I don't know what to say."

"It's okay. It's fine," Ivy said. "It was fun while it lasted, but I've never really been a long-term relationship person anyway."

I couldn't have dreamed up a more serendipitous direction for this conversation if I tried. Ivy didn't hate me. She had come to apologize to *me*. If I was dreaming, I just hoped I wouldn't get pinched any time soon.

"So . . . we're okay?" I asked, finally looking up again.

Ivy lifted a shoulder. "I don't love the way you went behind my back, but I think I can get past it. Eventually."

I pressed my lips together and nodded. "Are you coming in, then?"

Ivy glanced past me at the chapel. I could sense her hesitation and wondered what was causing it. If she was okay with me, why wouldn't she be okay with our sisters?

"Yeah. Sure," she said. "Why not?"

She gave me a tight smile as she walked past me up the steps. I felt like I should try to hug her or pat her on the back or something, but everything I thought of felt awkward, so I just let her go. As she got to the doorway, a stiff wind blew the skirt of her coat up and out around her and for a moment my heart stopped. Her dark silhouette against the white wall of the church was like something out of a gothic novel. Or a horror movie.

I took a breath and the moment passed. I knew I was just feeling antsy about the tentativeness of our relationship. About the inkling that someone might be out there watching us. That at any moment the Billings alumni might storm from the woods and try to shut us down again.

But then we were inside, enveloped in the warmth of a hundred candles and greeted by the smiles and hollers of our friends. And I knew then that everything was going to be okay.

THUMP IN THE NIGHT

"All right everyone, our first order of business is the new Billings Literary Society crest," I said, closing the book on the floor in front of me. "Kiki? Let's see what you've got."

Kiki had slicked all her hair back from her face and outlined her eyes in dark kohl pencil, making them appear so huge she almost looked like an anime character. Which, considering her obsession with the Japanese art form, might have been the point. She reached into her black messenger bag and pulled out a large sketchbook, which she laid flat on the floor in the center of the circle. With the flick of one finger she opened it up to a center page. Everyone gasped and leaned forward, balancing on knees and fingertips to get a better look.

"Kiki! That's so cool!" Amberly said, looking up with awe. Preppy, darling little Amberly had always regarded our resident creative punk Kiki with fear and awe, but this was different. She was impressed. We all were.

The crest was similar to the original, but sharper at the edges, the points taller, thinner, and more severe. Instead of dozens of entwined roses at the center, the crest was filled by one, extraordinarily intricate rose, the letters *BLS* were entwined in its details. So entwined that, unless you were looking for them, you might not see them. It was perfect. Headmaster Hathaway would be on the lookout for anything he could connect back to Billings, but he wouldn't be able to parse the letters here.

"What do you think, Reed?" Kiki asked, her eyes wide, ready and willing to be critiqued.

"I love it," I replied, feeling all warm and fuzzy inside. "You did an incredible job."

Kiki beamed, toying with the open men's tie she wore slung around the collar of her white shirt. "I thought it came out kind of rad."

"We can definitely use this," I said, pulling the sketchbook toward me.

"Use it? For what?" Noelle asked. "Are we all going to sew patches on all our clothes or something?"

Everyone chuckled, but a few of them looked at me nervously.

"No. I'm not going to make you trash your couture," I said, earning a relieved brow-wipe from Portia. Everyone laughed. "I was thinking we could use it as a subtle way to let the school know we're out there. Like, we could post it around campus or something. What do you guys think?"

Noelle sat forward and raised a hand. "Uh, I think it's an idiotic idea."

My face stung like she'd just thrown a vat of boiling water at me.

Ivy scoffed and shook her head. "Do you ever think Reed's ideas are good?"

"Yeah. When they're actually good," Noelle replied, glancing across her right shoulder at Ivy. Then she looked back at me, her chin tucked. "Reed, I thought the whole point of this secret-society thing was to remain a secret. Now you want to broadcast Kiki's— admittedly cool—logo all over campus? Why? Do you want to lead Double H directly to our doors?"

"No. Of course not. But this is what secret societies do," I said, crossing my arms over my chest. "If we post this in a few spots around campus, it'll get people wondering, get them talking. Give us some cache."

"I thought you didn't care about cache anymore," Noelle replied, mimicking my pose. "I thought this was all about friendship and sisterhood."

"It is, but—"

"I think it's a fab idea," Vienna said. "I *love* when I know stuff other people don't."

"We could post it on the announcement board, but bury it a little, so people will think it was there for a while," Lorna suggested.

"And maybe we can chalk it on the side of Hell Hall or something. Then when it rains or snows it'll get all drippy and abstract and spooky . . ." Tiffany said, leaning back on her hands with a grin.

Everyone started talking at once, throwing out ideas for places to plant the logo. Noelle grew increasingly tense.

"See? They like it," I said to Noelle.

"You guys," Noelle said loudly. There was no response. If anything, the chatter grew louder. She shoved herself to her feet, stepping on Amberly's pinky in the process. Amberly snatched her hand away and sucked on her flattened finger, shooting a pained look up at Noelle. "Ladies!" Noelle shouted.

They fell silent. Everyone looked at me first, then at Noelle, tipping their chins back to see her.

"Look, I'm all for having a little fun. You know that. But haven't we been warned enough already?" she said. "Do you really want to risk getting caught? They already bulldozed our house. Who knows what else they'll do to teach us a lesson?"

I stood up to face her. "Since when are you scared of anything?"

Her eyes narrowed as she looked me up and down. "I'm not scared. But I have been arrested once already, booted out of school, and left back a year . . . all in the process of saving *your* ass, so maybe my perspective is just a *tad* different than yours."

"Saving my ass?" I blurted, stepping forward. Kiki whipped her sketchbook with the precious crest in it out from under my feet. "We already went over this, Noelle. You were arrested because you assaulted my boyfriend!"

"Yeah, which no one would have ever known about if I hadn't been forced to go up to the roof and save you from that freak show Ariana!" Noelle countered, earning a few gasps from around the circle. "What were you thinking going up to the roof anyway? Were you high?"

"I was *trying* to make a phone call," I replied, my voice growing louder. "When you find out that your four best friends are total sadistic psychos who tied the love of your life to a pole and left him for dead, you kind of want to talk it out with someone!"

"Wait. I thought Josh was the love of your life," Ivy piped up.

My face burned with humiliation as I looked down at her. "He . . . he is. He just . . . I mean, Thomas was my *first* love. I—"

She lifted a hand as if to wave me off. "Just wanted to be clear."

"Oh, so now I'm a sadistic psycho?" Noelle blurted, ignoring the interjection. She took a step toward me, getting right in my face. "Who do you think you—"

A sudden bang stopped her mid rant. My heart vaulted into my throat. On the floor, my friends reached out and grabbed one another, terrified.

"What was that?" I whispered, crouching to their level. Noelle did the same, looking wildly around the room.

"It came from outside," she hissed. "Someone's out there."

Quickly, Tiffany, Rose, and Astrid snuffed out several of the candles. Suddenly every inch of my skin throbbed with fear.

Another bang. Closer this time. Amberly shrieked in fear, curling into Tiffany's side and clutching the arm of her sweater.

"Omigod. Omigodomigodomigod," Vienna said, rocking forward and back at an alarming pace. "What *is* that?"

"It's probably just the Billings alumni again," I whispered, not knowing what to believe. "I'll go outside. I'll go talk to them."

"Reed, no!" Ivy hissed, grabbing for my ankle as I started to rise. "Don't go out there."

"Why not?" I asked, somehow speaking past the tremendous lump of black fear lodged in my throat.

"What if it's not them?" Rose squeaked. "What if it's . . . something else?"

And then, a stiff wind whistled through the broken windows and doused the rest of the candles.

"Omigod! Reed!" Amberly whimpered.

I felt her fingers scrabble for mine in the dark. I couldn't see a thing. Not one inch in front of my face.

Another bang. Everyone screamed this time, even me. Then came the unmistakable sound of scuffling footsteps.

"Who's there?" I shouted.

Someone was crying. Someone else mewling like a cat. Then someone struggled to their feet in the dark.

"Ow!" Ivy shouted.

"What the—?"

Another scream, but this time it was far away. Outside maybe?

"What the hell was that?" Kiki asked, sounding like a five-year-old version of herself.

The loudest bang yet. Someone hugged me from the side, breathing heavily in my ear.

"Reed? Are you there?" Lorna whispered.

"WTH is going on?" Portia said.

"I'm here," I said. I held my breath for a long, long time. Everything was silent. Silent. Silent.

"Who has a candle?" I said finally.

"I do."

Tiffany crawled forward, finding first my knee, then my hand, with her fingers. She pressed the candle into my hand. I reached around to the back pocket of my jeans and fumbled out a pack of matches. I took Lorna's hand off my sleeve and handed her the candle.

"Take this and don't move."

In the pitch black, with my hands shaking, it took ten tries to light the match. When I finally did, Lorna's face loomed before me in the light, her bottom lip trembling as she held the candle toward me. I lit the wick, shook out the match, and took the candle away.

"Is everyone all right?" I asked. I slowly rose to my feet, my knees trembling in protest, as I held the candle and slowly turned in a circle. Ivy, who was curled up in a ball on the floor, slowly lifted her head. Tears streaked down her face.

"What the hell just happened?" she asked.

Astrid crawled out from behind the pulpit. Rose and Vienna only now released their grip on each other. Tentatively, everyone stood around me, taking deep breaths, checking over their shoulders.

"I don't know," I said. "Maybe it was just someone playing a prank? Could it have been Missy and those girls?"

"No. Missy?" Lorna said. "I don't think she'd—"

"Um, Reed?" Tiffany said loudly, her voice strained.

"What?" My heart thumped in fear.

Tiffany looked around at all of us. At Ivy and Rose, Portia and Lorna, Kiki and Astrid, Vienna and Amberly and me. Her eyes were wide with fear as she stepped forward.

"Where's Noelle?"

VANISHED

"Noelle!"

"Noelle! Are you out there!"

"Noelle! This is not funny! If you're hiding somewhere . . ."

"Everyone spread out," I said, my heart beating wildly in terror. "Maybe she tried to hide and fell or something."

Amberly hugged herself tightly. "Spread out? But what if whoever was out there is still—"

"Amberly! Just go!" I shouted.

I turned and headed for the alcove at the side of the building. Ivy came with.

"Reed, maybe it's okay," Ivy said, stepping carefully down the few steps to the main floor. "Maybe she just ran."

"What do you mean, ran?" I blurted, shoving aside an old dusty curtain. All that was behind it was a pile of tattered old bibles and mouse-chewed wicker baskets.

"She was just talking about not wanting to get caught," Ivy pointed out. "Maybe she figured it was the headmaster out there and she just bailed."

My heart sank at the very idea. "No," I said. "Not Noelle. She wouldn't just leave us here." Not the girl who had saved my life on the roof of Billings. The girl who'd whisked me off to St. Barths after Sabine turned on me, even though she was still mad that I'd hooked up with her sort-of boyfriend. The one who had lied directly to Headmaster Hathaway's face—to her father's friend's face—just to get us all out of trouble.

"Are you sure about that?" Ivy asked, raising her perfect black brows.

I was about to respond when Vienna and Portia returned from the hallway on the far side of the chapel.

"Anything?" I asked, my voice echoing throughout the room.

"Nothing," Portia replied.

"Astrid?" I asked as Astrid and Kiki emerged from the pastor's office.

"Door's still locked back there. Nothing's been moved," Astrid replied.

Slowly everyone returned from their search, their faces blank and scared.

"Why don't you just call her?" Ivy suggested. "Maybe she's walking back to campus right now."

I felt a jolt of hope and ran over to my bag, extracting my phone from the inside pocket and speed-dialing Noelle. It rang once. Then twice. Then, a ring tone started to play softly somewhere inside the room. I stopped breathing.

"Where is that coming from?"

Everyone started to look around, bending at the waist, checking under pews, holding their candles aloft. The floor creaked underfoot as we crept around, searching.

"Oh my God," Portia said suddenly.

"What?" I blurted.

She stood up from behind one of the pews. Hooked around her thumb was one of the thick straps of Noelle's black Chanel purse.

"Her stuff is strewn all over back here," Portia said.

I glanced at the spot where Noelle had been sitting, a good fifty feet from where her bag had been spilled. The white bakery box sat on its side, as if it had been tipped over in some kind of struggle. Slowly, I lowered my iPhone from my ear. Portia reached inside the bag and silenced Noelle's phone.

"Reed?" Amberly said shakily. "What does this mean?"

"I have no idea," I heard myself say. My voice sounded very far away. "No idea at all."

THE GAME IS ON

We walked in silence back to campus, all of us together in one tight knot. There was no way I was telling these girls to split up now. No way I was going to risk another one of them—or more—disappearing into the night. I no longer cared about getting caught by the Billings alumni committee or by Hathaway or by anyone else.

I just wanted everyone to be safe.

The whole way down the hill, I held my phone in my hand, waiting for it to sing out. Even though Noelle's phone was tucked away in her bag, which was slung over my forearm, I willed her to call somehow. Maybe she was back at campus already, which meant she could use one of the ancient pay phones. Or borrow someone's cell. Or break into Hell Hall and use one of the phones there. Anything to let me know she was okay.

But the cell remained silent.

When we arrived at the north side of Bradwell, we paused and loosened our grips on one another a bit. No one knew what to say, where to go, how to act. The wind whistled overhead, rustling the topmost branches of the bare, spindly trees and all I could think was, *Noelle is out there somewhere. . . . But where?*

"I'll call you guys if I hear from her," I whispered, trying to look each of them in the eye. "I'm sure she's okay."

No I'm not. I'm not. I'm not.

"Just go back to your rooms. It's going to be fine."

Slowly, reluctantly, the group started to disband. Amberly slipped through the back door of Bradwell, while the rest of us broke into two clusters—Kiki, Vienna, Astrid, Rose, Tiffany, and Portia headed for Parker, while Lorna, Ivy, and I turned our steps toward Pemberly.

"Do you really think it's going to be fine?" Lorna whispered, looping her arm around mine.

"It's Noelle," I said, forcing a smile. "When is Noelle ever not fine?"

Lorna smiled slightly, but Ivy shot me a look over her head. Like I should be honest. Like I should tell Lorna how scared I felt. Well, I disagreed. No one needed to feel any more worried and uncertain than they already did. As we approached the back door of Pemberly, I kept hoping that Noelle would pop out from behind one of the shrubs or jump out from around the corner and shout, "Gotcha, Glass-Licker!" I kept bracing for it, like it could come at any second. And then I'd yell at her and we'd laugh and hug and everything would be okay.

But she never did.

Ivy used her key card to open our dorm. Lorna finally let go of me as we stepped into the well-lit lobby.

If she doesn't call or show up by the time I get to my room, I'm calling the police, I told myself. We parted at the stairs, Lorna continuing on up to the room she shared with Constance. Ivy and I paused outside our doors.

"Want me to come in for a while? We could wait together," Ivy said.

"No. It's okay," I told her.

Because Noelle is already inside. She's going to jump out and scare the crap out of me and I don't want you there when she does it.

I hope. I hope, hope, hope.

"Okay, then," Ivy said, placing her hand on the doorknob of her door. She reached over and gave me a one-armed hug. "I'm sure she's fine. She's probably just enjoying making us sweat."

"Yeah," I croaked.

With a bolstering smile, Ivy went inside and closed the door quietly behind her. I turned and placed my hands flat on my door, resting my forehead between them.

"Please just be inside," I whispered. "Please, Noelle."

I held my breath and opened the door.

"Hey!"

My heart leapt, but it wasn't Noelle. Josh was kicked back on my bed, the desk light on, reading a folded-over paperback.

"Where were you?" he asked, laying his book aside with a smile. "You cheating on me already?" he joked.

I started to cry. His face fell.

"Oh, hey. Bad joke," he said, getting up and wrapping me up in his arms. "I guess we shouldn't joke about cheating, considering how we broke up. . . ."

"It's not that."

I buried my face in his sweater, letting my bag and Noelle's fall to the floor with a thump.

"Then what is it?" he asked, cupping my face in both his hands and tilting it up. "Reed, what's wrong?"

How was I going to explain this to him? Where did I start? Should I reveal all about the Billings Literary Society up-front? He was not going to like it. Josh had hated Billings from the beginning, and I'm sure that he was relieved the house was gone. If he knew I'd started it up again, and that apparently starting it up had put me in danger, he was going to lose it.

"It's Noelle," I said finally, my voice breaking. "She's—"

Suddenly, my phone beeped. Or was it Noelle's phone? I dropped to the floor, scrambling around frantically, dumping the entire contents of our bags out onto the floor. Noelle's phone was silent. Dark. But where the hell was mine?

"Looking for this?" Josh asked.

He crouched down and stood up with my phone in his hand. The screen was lit up with a text.

"It fell out of your pocket," he said. "It's a text."

He did a double take as he looked at the screen, his green eyes frightened. "Reed? What the hell is this?" he asked.

I snatched the phone away from him. It was a long text, all in capital letters, and as I read it, my insides slowly turned to ice-cold granite.

WE HAVE NOELLE LANGE. IF YOU GO TO THE POLICE, SHE DIES. IF YOU GO TO HER FAMILY, SHE DIES. IF YOU GO TO THE HEADMASTER, SHE DIES. YOU WILL FOLLOW OUR EVERY INSTRUCTION TO THE LETTER, OR SHE WILL DIE. THE GAME IS ON, REED BRENNAN. THE PRIZE? NOELLE'S LIFE.

From bestselling author
KATE BRIAN

♥ ♥ ♥ ♥ ♥

Juicy reads for the **sweet** and the **sassy**!

Sweet 16
As seen in *CosmoGIRL*!

Lucky T
"Fans of Meg Cabot's *The Princess Diaries* will enjoy it."—*SLJ*

Fake Boyfriend
"Full of humor and drama."—*VOYA*

The Virginity Club
"*Sex and the City: High School Edition.*"—*KLIATT*

The Princess & the Pauper
"Truly exceptional chick-lit."—*Kirkus Reviews*

Ally Ryan is about to discover that it turns out you can go home again, but it will pretty much suck.

The first book in a new series about losing it all and being better off, from author Kieran Scott.